COBBLE

COBBLE

Eric S. Brown &
Susanne Brydenbaugh

Mundania Press

A Mundania Press Production

Mundania Press LLC
6470A Glenway Avenue, #109
Cincinnati, Ohio 45211-5222

To order additional copies of this book, contact:
books@mundania.com
www.mundania.com

Cover Art © 2005 by Trace Edward Zaber
Cover layout by Stacey L. King
Book Design and Production by Daniel J. Reitz, Sr.
Marketing and Promotion by Bob Sanders
Edited by Jennifer Scholz

Trade Paperback ISBN-10: 1-59426-228-4
Trade Paperback ISBN-13: 978-1-59426-228-9

eBook ISBN-10: 1-59426-229-2
eBook ISBN-13: 978-978-1-59426-229-6

First Edition • September 2005

Library of Congress Catalog Card Number 2005934686

Production by Mundania Press LLC
Printed in the United States of America

10   9   8   7   6   5   4   3   2   1

Introduction

Kiss The Count Good-Bye
by Mark McLaughlin

Back when I was growing up, I had very Old World tastes when it came to my reading selections.

I used to sit in a local library on weekend afternoons and read well-worn old hardbound anthologies with stories by such authors as Arthur Machen, H.G. Wells, Oliver Onions, J. Sheridan LeFanu, Bram Stoker, M.R. James, H.R. Wakefield and Ambrose Bierce. Those grand old gentlemen, all long departed, wrote about quaint, creepy terrors, like slowly shambling mummies, midnight pagan rituals, wicked gnomes, vampire royalty, invisible creatures, ghostly maidens and scheming warlocks casting ancient spells...

Like I said: quaint. A little creepy, but not the sort of matters that would frighten any of us these days.

Folks in our modern world don't worry about sprites and phantoms and ectoplasmic hauntings, No indeed.

Those sorts of Gothic goings-on went out of style with the last episode of *Dark Shadows*.

Now people are worried about...oh, let's see...

Stalkers. Serial killers. Hit-and-run drivers. Mad cow disease. Sudden Infant Death Syndrome. Flesh-eating bacteria. AIDS. The Ebola virus. Toxins in the air and in our food. Radon. Radioactivity. Nuclear war. Global annihilation.

Our high-gloss world is loaded with high-tech dangers, and the only phantoms you'll find floating around us are the broad-daylight specters of random violence, lingering disease and apocalyptic doom.

Those cheery notions bring us to the book you are holding in your hands.

It's a horror novel, but you won't find any mummies, witches, warlocks, vampires or any other dusty old hobgoblins.

This is a book of real-life horrors.

Of course, now you may be saying: excuse me, but it features zombies, right? The living dead? Real-life, you say? Haven't seen any mobile cadavers strolling Dawn-Of-The-Dead-style through the mall lately, okay?

Yeah, you got me there. You're right. Zombies don't exist.

But as a metaphor for the combined phobias of today's fear-fraught world, they can't be beat. Think about it...

They are violent—they'll take one look at you and rip your face-skin right off your skull.

They are sickness incarnate—a walking epidemic. A plague with teeth. And they won't stop until they've shared their virulent, lethal contagion with you.

They are full-time agents of the Apocalypse. Count Dracula may take an evening here and there to socialize at dinner parties, and werewolves may even hold down day jobs (maybe at pet stores, so they can get employee discounts on chew toys and flea collars). But zombies are no-nonsense, hell-bent for destruction, rampaging, slavering, two-legged leviathans of pure evil.

So don't invite them to your next party or give them jobs at your office. Not even as temps.

The co-authors of this book have done an excellent and thorough job of combining many of the fears of today's complex world into one high-energy adventure.

So if you like gentle, leisurely Victorian stories of the supernatural, that's fine—they can be entertaining in a nostalgic sort of way. But if you think horror begins and ends with tuxedo-clad European bloodsuckers and ivy-shrouded, mysterious castles surrounded by howling wolves—it's time to kiss the Count goodbye...

Because the zombies have arrived.

The World of Cobble Timeline

March 10th, 2007: First corpse reanimates in a rural village in India, destroyed by villagers.

April 30th, 2007: Nearly 100 corpses in scattered locales around the globe reanimate.

May 1st, 2007: Media coverage of the phenomena begins.

May 2nd, 2007: The Center for Disease Control, among other agencies, begins to investigate the cause of this reanimation.

May 13th, 2007: Wide outbreaks of reanimates begin to occur worldwide.

May 13th, 2007: Africa in chaos, state of emergency declared by Japan, United Kingdom, and former Soviet Union.

May 14th, 2007: Outbreaks reach epidemic levels. United States declares a state of martial law.

May 15th, 2007: The first battle for New York occurs between US military forces and the reanimates.

June 1st, 2007: 98% of all major cities in the continental United States now overrun, rural areas first beginning to experience the level of trouble with the reanimates that the cities faced in the early days of the virus. Second battle of New York occurs. Texas also now ruled a dead zone. June 12th, 2007: Presidential Press conference. Announcement made to use nuclear weapons against major infected zones.

June 12th, 2007: Center of Disease control reports that the reanimates are caused by virus of unknown origins. Means of transmission not fully understood but a bite or wound inflicted by a carrier causes infection within minutes (hours in stronger individuals). CDC continues work on a vaccine against the plague.

June 12th, 2007: First reanimates occur on Cobble Island.

June 13th, 2007: Led by local sheriff, citizens of Cobble Island instrument a plan to keep the plague in check on the island. Islanders put down main uprising of reanimates in island cemetery.

June 13th, 2007: Over a dozen major cities in the United States are hit by nuclear strikes.

June 30th, 2007: President killed in attempt to flee Washington, DC, Vice President sworn in. Second round of nuclear strikes hit American cities. Remaining units of United State military are scattered and out of communication with command.

June 30th, 2007: Last communication with countries outside of United States. It is assumed that no one remains alive in the 3rd world countries, Australia is considered lost, United Kingdom reports in last communication to have followed US example of nuclear weapons use.

July 4th, 2007: Continental United States now a post-apocalyptic wasteland. Most civilians are dead, world population of total non-infected humans below five hundred million. Primary survivors are bands of looters and military personnel.

July 7th, 2007: Military unit lead by Captain Elliot Simon abandons post, heads East.

July 28th, 2007: Captain Simon and Dr. Paxton, a lead genetic researcher, decide to leave United States mainland and begin preparations.

August 4th, 2007: Simon's unit disembarks, via a fleet of looted helicopters, for Cobble Island.

I

Something moved in the water towards the horizon. Jared raised the binoculars he held in his well wrinkled hands and saw a tiny motor boat beaten and tossed about by the waves.

"Trouble?" Shannon asked, flicking his tongue over his thick lips in anticipation.

Sweat beaded on Jared's brow. Unlike Shannon, he dreaded standing watch. The faces of those he turned away haunted him in his dreams. Logically, he knew the island could only support so many but it did nothing to ease his pain at those he sentenced to exile. His professional oath was to save lives not complicate them or cut them short; he had been—in fact still was though long retired—a doctor.

The boat drew closer to the dock. Its motor was silent and burnt out. Abroad it, a man paddled desperately to reach them. Two small children huddled near him beneath a dingy-grey blanket, shivering and wet, faces pale in the half-moon light.

They were close enough now for Shannon and Jared to see them. A young girl, no older than seven held a younger boy's hand, murmurs of comfort and the strain of a smile despite the fact that they could see the rifle each man held to his side. The younger man pumped a round into the chamber of his 12 gauge and walked down the dock to meet them. Pointing his own rifle downward, Jared sighed inwardly and followed.

As they approached the boat, the man struggled to secure it to the dock and the children stared at them with half-dead eyes. The man looked up at them smiling.

"Thank God," he sighed, "oh thank God, we made it."

Shannon leveled his shotgun at the man's chest. "You can't stay. We're full up here. Best you turn that boat around and head back the way you came."

Jared watched as the realization of Shannon's words sunk in and the man's smile crumbled from his face.

"What?" the man stammered, "You can't mean that. We don't have any food or fuel. My children..."

Shannon cut him off. "Not our problem is it? Ya seem to be able to use that paddle pretty well. This is the last time I am tellin' ya to start usin' it again."

The man stood there for a moment then reached for something buried inside his jacket. Shannon's 12 gauge thundered. Blood sprayed the dock as the man toppled backwards splashing into the water below.

"Jesus!" Jared heard himself yell.

Shannon whirled on him. "Ya know the rules Doc. That bastard was goin' for a gun as sure I'm still breathing."

"We'll never know what he was going for now will we?" Jared snapped. The night was silent except for the waves crashing against the shore until a weak sobbing drew Jared's eyes back to the boat.

"What about them?" he asked pointing at the children. "Are you going to murder them too?"

The children were standing now, the girl sheltering the boy's face in her shoulder. Jared saw that both had dark red hair, curly, and tousled from long days at sea. The blanket had slid to a heap at their bare feet. Their soaked clothes clung to their tiny, mal-nourished bodies and their breath was visible in the cool air.

Shannon stood considering the children; Jared could see the wheels turning in his cramped little mind.

And after a few seconds, "Now, Doc, what do you take me for? Marta will take them in. She always does."

Jared moved toward the boat to do what he could for them. "Terry's going to be pissed with you Shannon and the next watch is going to have to finish cleaning up your mess when that guy comes crawling back out of the water."

"To Hell with Terry," Shannon cursed, lighting up a cigarette. "If he did his job we wouldn't be out here freezing our asses off to begin with."

Jared clenched his teeth together and let the cold air defuse the anger; there would be another time. It would serve no purpose to confront Shannon, not here and not now with the children to care for. He put the rifle down on the planks of the dock and held an arm out to the children. They shrank back in the boat; the boy's face turned toward the sea, clutching desperately at his sister's waist. The boat rocked precariously from their movement and Jared backed off a step, decided they needed more assurance that he wasn't the monster that Shannon had proven to be.

"I'm not going to hurt you. I promise. There's a lady here on the island, she'll take care of you. I'll take you to her."

And still the girl stared at the place where her father had just stood, shell-shocked eyes and tremors racked her body, but her shoulders were straight, her chin defiant. Jared couldn't help but notice she had more courage than most men he knew. Yet, how pathetic they looked, huddled in the boat's stern, unsure of their fate. Never, as long as he lived, would he get used to seeing children displaced and devastated.

Jared tried a different approach. "Where you from?" not really expecting an answer, he continued, "I'm from Texas. Ever heard of the place?"

Silence.

Shannon shuffled his feet, his mind already occupied with Gina's stew that she'd promised earlier that afternoon. "Just pick 'em up and bring 'em on. Our shift's almost over and I'm hungry."

Jared waved him away. "Go on without me. I'll see to this."

Shannon was relieved. He didn't care to spend the next half hour trekking over to Marta's place where she would delay them another hour with questions. He'd done his good deed for the day: the island was safe; the children were still alive—though it meant two extra mouths to feed. And if he'd saw fit to spare the brats, surely the other man could take it from here. "Okay, then. See ya around," and he turned without a backwards glance and made his way down the dirt road leaving Jared just as relieved to be rid of him.

He turned his attention back to the children. "I'm sorry about your father. It's..." and he searched in vain for the words that wouldn't trivialize the murder they had just witnessed, realized there were no words, but he had to give them something, "...not supposed to happen that way."

Jared eased his legs over to the side of the small boat. It swayed as he held to the sides and climbed in. A whimper came from the little boy, but he still didn't turn his head to face Jared, just squeezed his sister tighter and the girl looked wistfully to the sea as Jared held his breath and sat down in the bottom of the boat in the stern. He prayed they wouldn't see the cold waves as their only option. His medical mind listed the complications of diving into the cold water—hypothermia; the fierce undertow; the encompassing dark and murkiness of the sea. If only he could win them over so that they didn't see him as a threat. And again he coaxed, "I'm not going to hurt you. I wouldn't have hurt your father, either." Then almost to his self, "We would've come to some rational decision. The plague makes some people so scared that they do bad things. They just can't trust other folks anymore."

The girl's voice, too strong it seemed to come from such a small body, rose from the boat. "He's gone. Forever."

Jared didn't think 'forever' was quite right, but he nodded. "I'm sorry. I'm sorry as I can be—but you have to trust me to take care of you. I'll take you some place warm where there are other kids just like you. Or," and he hesitated, hoped he was making the right call, "I'll let you and your brother do what you have to do. I'll get out of the boat right now—but I don't want to; I want to help you. Wouldn't you like to get something to eat first?"

By degrees the small boy's head turned to Jared and the girl looked down at him, surprised. His thumb went to his mouth and he glanced from Jared to the floor of the boat.

"My name is Jared. What's yours?"

"His name's Isaac," the girl said. "He doesn't talk, not since..."

Jared bit his lip. *Not since the world went crazy.*

"My name is Ingrid," and for the first time the girl looked away as if the disclosure of her name made her vulnerable. "We're from Massachusetts. It was snowing when we left."

Jared smiled. "I've visited Massachusetts once." He held his arm up over his head, "Snow up to here."

Seconds ticked by. "Ingrid, I've given you my promise and I never break my promises. Are the two of you ready to get out of this cold?"

She said nothing, but eased closer. Reaching down she picked up the threadbare blanket, gathered it around the boy's shoulders and took Isaac's tiny hand into her own.

⌘

The mid-day sun rested at its peak in the sky. Heat shimmered in waves from the road as Amy made her way home. She hated this time of year when she woke up shivering in the cold and then roasted in days that seemed hotter than those of the summer so recently past. She carried a large sack of groceries from the island's general store and shifted her burden awkwardly as she looked around at the town she called home. Despite all the horrors it and the world had been through so little had changed here. The street was still filled with people going about their daily lives. Old man Jackson sat outside the town meeting hall and waved at her as she walked by. She returned his wave as best she could. The only noticeable difference in life on Cobble was that no one drove except her father and his deputies. There simply wasn't enough gas anymore. Everyone walked or biked now. However, it was times like these, as she huffed up the small hill towards the edge of town to the small house she shared with her father, that she missed driving the most.

Her father's patrol car was parked in the drive, so she headed around to the back door not wanting to disturb him if he were asleep and walked quietly into the kitchen. She placed the groceries on the counter top and started spreading them out to be put away when Terry staggered into the kitchen from the living room. He rubbed his eyes and plopped down in a chair at the table.

"Hi, Dad. Dinner won't be ready for a bit. I just got home."

Dark circles lined his bloodshot eyes as he splayed his hands on the table top, studied the freckles that were turning to age spots. Curious that as time went by his hands looked more and more like someone else's. He could say that about the rest of him too, his legs, and arms…his face and the moustache that had long since turned silvery-grey.

"You ok?"

Terry shrugged. "Nothing I can't get through, I suppose." He folded his hands away and put them in his lap. "We had incomers last night, a father and his two children."

Amy put the bread in the cupboard. "Oh? So did the Council decide to let them stay?" She spoke of the town council who decided such issues. Children almost always were allowed to stay, and if an adult had a certain skill to benefit the island and its society, the council would grant them refuge also. Unfortunately, more than half of the adults were turned away. There simply weren't enough resources to take in everyone and they had to take up the Women and Children First policy.

Terry paused. "Marta took the two children in."

"Of course she did." Amy grinned, but noticed her father's tense expression remained.

Terry closed his eyes and sighed heavily. "They came in on Jared and Shannon's watch."

Her response was automatic. "Oh no." She knew then there was more to her father's anxiety than limited resources.

Terry pursed his lips. "Shannon fired point blank at the children's father."

Amy placed a hand to her stomach and listened as her father continued.

"I got two versions of the story—and once again Shannon gets away with breaking the law by pleading self defense. Mayor Beck sits back and practically pats the little punk on the back." He slapped the table top with the palm of his hand causing Amy to jump. "You would think the sheriff would be able to enforce the laws, but they tie my hands. Beck and his constituents encourage defiance."

Amy had heard it all before. It was the same divisive problem that had prevailed since the island was founded, with half the population wanting to ban mainland refugees—some even wanted to turn away the children—and the other half approved letting the elect council make the tough decisions.

"I just wish your mother was here. I could sure use her wisdom at times like these.

"You're pushing yourself too hard, Dad. Everybody on this island knows you are doing the best you can under the circumstances, even Shannon, though he would never admit it."

Terry grunted non-commitably as Amy joined him at the table. "I miss Mom too, but no matter how you kill yourself to keep the rest of us safe, no matter if you make this island a paradise; Mom's not coming back."

"It's more than just your Mother. I feel like I am trying to stop the end of the world."

Amy broke into a loving smile. She stood up and embraced her father tightly. "Everything's going to work out Dad. You'll see. We've made it this far haven't we?"

Terry's face tightened in an attempt to smile back. "I..."

The radio on his belt cut him off crackling to life. "Terry, if you're there, please respond."

Terry motioned Amy to silence. "What is it, Gordon? This had better be important. I was just about to have dinner with my daughter for once."

"You don't know?" Gordon's shocked static filled voice echoes through the kitchen.

"Know what?"

The distant sound of whirling blades cut the air out-side. Terry dropped his radio and ran outside the back porch with Amy following in his foot steps. Together they stared in awe at the sky. A huge, high-tech helicopter of obvious military make hovered on the horizon. Dark and foreboding, it was a symbol of what they had left behind in the old world—an intrusion of past souring the present harmony they'd struggled to attain and keep. As they watched in petrified silence, the helicopter was joined by two others. The three transports turned in the air and headed out toward the vast and rural farmlands of Cobble Island.

"Sweet Jesus," Terry muttered under his breath. "What the Hell is going on?"

A high-pitch screech erupted overhead as a twin pair of Apaches streaked over his house following in the wake of the transports.

"Dad?" Amy asked in a quivering voice.

Terry was already racing for his car. "Go in the house. Lock the doors and don't let anyone in unless it's me."

"Dad! Be careful!"

Terry slammed the door of the patrol car and fired up the engine. The car's wheels squealed and threw gravel as he dove-tailed out onto the road heading for town.

Inside the lead helicopter above Cobble, Captain Elliot Simon smiled. He looked out the window at the small town below surrounded by fields of growing crops and distant farm houses and silos. The island was everything the ru-mors spoke of and more; more than he'd dared to dream. Sergeant McClure, a jaded veteran of the war against the risen dead, sat near him. The sergeant's face was an un-readable mask of scarred and grizzled flesh even to Simon. McClure's eyes were hard as he leaned forward to yell over the copter's roaring engine. "I don't think the natives are too happy to see us!"

Simon scoffed. "Too bad for them."

Outside the town hall, a mass of frightened and angry islanders had gathered. As soon as Terry pulled the pa-trol car to a halt and opened his door, he was besieged by questions from every front. Standing towards the back of the crowd, an aged man in a fine suit leaned on a hand-made cane stared at him with a pleading gaze. Terry fought his way through the mass of people to the man. Mayor Beck extended his hand. "It's good to see you, Terry. How you holdin' up?"

"Been better."

Shannon walked up to the pair grinning. "Can't wait to see how you handle this one, Sheriff."

Mayor Beck turned to a young man in the crowd. "Robert, we're going to need the trucks. Get them ready."

Before the plague Robert had owned the sole gas-station on the island and was now the island's only source for fuel. Luck would have it that Cobble being a tourist trap in better days had been prepared for the usual on-slaught of crowds wanting to rent boats and go sight-seeing around the island so Robert had been stocked up for a season that never came. Though his supply was running low after months of rationed use, he still had plenty left for this and he couldn't think of better a cause to break into his stash. He turned and ran down towards his place on the docks.

Less than a half an hour later, a convoy of pick-ups led by Terry's patrol car streaked up along Sheridan road towards Halsbrook field where the fleet of birds had landed leaving a cloud of dust in their wake. Armed men filled the back of each pick-up and tensions were running high. Not one among them knew what to expect or what they would be facing.

Out in Halsbrook field, Captain Simon was busy giving orders. All twelve of his copters had landed and were accounted for. Men and women were scurrying about trying to establish a perimeter and a makeshift base camp. Already command and supply tents were being staked up. In all, Simon's group consisted of about thirty troops. Most were either Special Forces or pilots and there was only one civilian among them; a young doctor named Gil Paxton. The good Doctor was Simon's other hope for the future whether or not his plan for the island worked out. Paxton had been the lead researcher in a cure for the plague and even now, under Simon's watchful eye, continued searching for a way to break the plague's terrible rule over the Earth.

McClure pointed to the winding road leading to the field. He and Simon watched the convoy of trucks approaching. Lieutenant Christina Hannigan, a tough though attractive woman, and pilot Michael Drake, a young man who appeared to be in his early twenties and carried himself with a cat like grace, joined them. McClure looked as if he almost pitied the locals on the way to the field. "Nothing we can't handle, sir," He assured Simon.

"Take care of them carefully, Lieutenant. I don't believe our good sergeant is capable of handling this delicate situation." Simon ordered Christina, ignoring McClure's comment. McClure shot him a look of disapproval then stomped off to supervise a pair trying to unload Doctor Paxton's equipment from a nearby copter.

"I don't want any bloodshed unless absolutely necessary, understood?" Simon continued.

"Loud and clear, sir," Christina nodded.

⁓⁓

Terry opened the door of his patrol car and got out with slow purpose. He held up his hand to the convoy. No one would fire unless he himself was fired upon. The men opened the doors of the trucks and jeeps and positioned their guns, waiting for their cue if necessary.

Terry would listen to what the men had to say, but relinquishing any supplies that they had would not be an option. He was determined to keep it on a civil level, if possible, but his gut feeling about it was there would be a clash for survival. Cobble had something the men wanted, or maybe they just wanted Cobble in its entirety. He wondered if the outside world was completely devastated by now, shriveled and maggot-ridden. Cobble would be a paradise, the only apple on a barren tree. Ripe for plucking. Time to find out, he guessed, and he took the safety mechanism off the rifle with his finger as he walked—those military types wouldn't fail to see that little warning.

Terry stopped in the center, red dust clouds swirling. Let them walk to me, he thought. Let them come to me with their overbearing pompous attitudes. It was still his island, his rules. And he mentally decided that if he was fired upon, he'd use his one shot to take down the man who appeared to be in charge. The one who stood with his legs braced apart and his hands behind his back, and who, even at this distance, had a hard edge about him.

A slim figure stood at the commander's side. Even in the baggy unisex fatigues, Terry could distinguish it as a woman. The commander listened to her as she spoke and pointed around the perimeter. And then he nodded, reluctantly, and took a couple of steps back.

The woman walked toward Terry, empty-handed until she took off the green camouflage cap, letting her white-blond hair glint under the sun. Nice strategy, he thought. It would be unlikely for them to shoot a woman with no weapon. This was the invader's act of good faith. Terry thought it smacked of cowardice.

She smiled as she neared. Not a girl-smile, no, more of a hostess smile. Polite and respectful. He didn't return the sentiment. Nor did he acknowledge the long-fingered hand that reached out to shake his—"I'm Lieutenant Christina Hannigan,"—and with a slight regret, lowered it to her side. "We're not here to cause trouble, I assure you," she turned and pointed to one of the helicopters in the distance. "With us, as our guest, is Dr. Gil Paxton, renowned scientist and biochemist. He has concluded that this island may hold a component in which a vaccination for the plague can be made." She paused to allow her words to take affect. "A cure for all our woes. A chance for the world."

Terry looked into her blue eyes. "There's nothing to save of the world anymore. You think I'm that gullible?"

The Lieutenant sighed, closed her eyes briefly. "And what about yourselves? Are you not worth saving?"

"Lady, Lieutenant who-ever-you-are, we don't have the plague here. And if it comes knocking we bury it deep and in so many pieces that God couldn't put 'em all back together again." He looked past her, to the surly commander. "And what's a scientist need with this sort of entourage— from the looks of you people, you're Special Forces. So tell me, what's Special Forces got to do with medicine?"

"Protection. What else?" she said and he could tell she was sincere in her belief in that moment. But he didn't trust the commander who would send a woman to do his politics. Didn't trust him at all.

"Look," she tried again. "How do we know that he *doesn't* need protection—the state of the world...it's all in shambles. No, it's dead. And the undead is all that's left. This man is our *only* hope." And a whispered plea: "Our only hope of survival—in the big sense—as a species. How long do you think you can hold out on this island? What of your children and grandchildren, and their right to existence?"

That had been the question on his mind for some time and it irked him to have to address it with this woman, an unwanted stranger. The call was not his alone to make. And he nodded, realizing things could be much worse— they could've come to take their island from them, could've made demands that would ensure bloodshed. "I'll call a council meeting tomorrow at one o'clock. You can come and make your case," and then he paused, "bring the doctor with you. I'm sure there will be questions only he can answer. But no one else will be admitted in. Do I make myself clear? You and the doctor." And he turned without giving her a chance to respond, walked back to the truck and signaled the convoy back into town where the questions would keep him busy for hours.

⤟⤞

The town meeting was held the next day. Everyone on the island showed up to discuss the new-comers, except for those assigned to "the watch" along the shores and now the secondary "watch" of keeping an eye on the military unit firmly encamped on Halsbrook field. Things went pretty well all things considered. Terry listened to circular arguments that seemed to drone on for hours and even had to set down into the crowd more than once to break up a few minor fist fights. Lt. Hannigan and Dr. Paxton explained the mission for the cure to the plague to the island folk, took questions and answered to the best of their ability. In the end though, it was decided the unit could stay on the island by the simple fact that no one wanted an all out war. It was true that the islanders greatly outnumbered the unit in terms of man power and "could" drive them off if the need arose *but* the unit was a group of professional killers and way outgunned the island folk. A battle between the two would leave far too many dead with most of the causalities being on the island-folk's side.

The unit hadn't requested much more than Terry had expected. Their demands were simple and seemingly easy to meet. They only wanted to be allowed residence to continue their work in finding a cure, a building of the islanders' choosing which could be turned into a full scale lab for their doctor, and the right to come to into town in small groups to trade for other needed supplies.

As the meeting closed, the islanders remained almost as divided as they had when they entered about the military presence but no one at least seemed on the verge of doing anything rash and more than a few, especially the shop owners were excited at the prospect of a new source of trade. Terry waited as the last of the township filtered through the doors, turned and faced the Lt. and doctor.

"Sounds like we have ourselves a peaceable arrangement," he dug his hands deep into his pockets. "You keep your side of the bargain, and I'll keep mine. That way it stays peaceful."

"Sheriff? A question if I might," Dr. Paxton said, taking off his round glasses and wiped the lenses with the front of his shirt. Terry nodded, crossed his arms in front of his chest.

"We're going to need a few men, preferably those that know the island well, to expedite the process." Dr Paxton didn't pause, but hurried on. "We've brought some extra supplies that could come in handy: freeze-dried meats, diesel fuel and kerosene. Not to mention medical goods like antibiotics."

Terry tried not to seem eager, but even a small amount of what he'd mentioned would go a long way...and if things improved in the mainland...if the plague was stopped, then more supplies could be scrounged up and the burden would lift considerably.

Terry nodded. "I'll see what I can do for you. I'm sure some will volunteer with those kinds of reimbursements. We live in a constant state of tight supply, as you probably have already gathered."

"Yes," Dr. Paxton said with a touch of a smile.

"Come on, I'll show you where you can set up your equipment. Cindy Dougherty, our seamstress, is going to stay with her sister and brother-in-law for the time being and she's going to let you use her home as quarters for your work—a very hospitable offer, if you ask me. I didn't even ask her to. Goes to show the good nature of us islanders."

The doctor didn't quite respond with the same good nature, Terry thought. He seemed preoccupied and "hmm" was all that was said in the face of the sacrifice Miss Dougherty was making. But Lt. Hannigan pushed forward and compensated with a blush and "Please give Ms. Dougherty our thanks for such a nice offer. We really appreciate it."

"Sure. Will do," Terry said and reached for the wide-brim hat on the bench. "We'll meet up tomorrow and I'll have your volunteers at that time; I'll show you to the Dougherty house, too, if you want to go ahead and have your stuff ready."

"Oh, everything is ready," Paxton said. "All ready to go when you are, *Sheriff*." But the condescension in his voice rattled Terry's nerves. Maybe he was just being overly sensitive, he thought. But things *were* moving faster than he liked. "Fine then. Good day to you," he managed a slight smile and turned on his heels, back straight and boots clicking rhythmically on the polished floor of the hall. *Yes, until tomorrow.* He hoped it was the right thing to do. But there was something about all of this that rubbed him the wrong way. There was something about the commander and the doctor that he just didn't trust but couldn't quite put his finger on. The lieutenant, she seemed sincere, but could he really be sure? Did he really have a choice at this point? The township had voted. They had guests to accommodate. And a plague to kill.

Terry headed home after the meeting. Amy was gone when he got there. He imagined she was out with her friends talking about the "new-comers" like everyone else on the island. He retrieved his half finished bottle of Vodka from its hiding place in his bedroom and settled into the living room recliner. He twisted off its top and took a long swallow from the bottle closing his eyes to the world. The phone in the kitchen rang at that exact moment. Cursing, he slammed the bottle down on the coffee table and went to answer it. When he said "Hello", it was Gordon's voice that answered.

"Gordon, what the Hell do you want?"

"I am sorry to bother you again, Terry, but..."

"Gordon, I don't give a damn what the military is up to..."

"Terry, it's not about that. It's Wiggins."

Terry felt his insides go cold. He had been dreading this moment and now it was here, at the worst possible time.

"His wife just called. He died a few minutes ago," Gordon continued on.

Terry shook his head sadly. "I'm on my way."

He hung up the phone and put on his hat.

≈∾≈

When he reached the Wiggins' house, he took a moment before getting out of the car. He stared at the cracking white paint on the banister of the porch and remembered all the times in his childhood he'd played in this yard. Mrs. Wiggins always had had lemonade and cookies for the boys who so many times had shattered her upstairs window playing softball in the large area of the front yard. The Wiggins' house was the closest farm to town and it had been the spot to play anything from touch football to baseball without having to hoof it all the way up into the island's farmland proper. Mr. Wiggins, like his wife, always viewed the boys, Terry included, with nothing but affection. Even back then, he had been old. But he played with them when he could and told them stories of "the war". As Terry had grown to adulthood, Mr. Wiggins had been there too. Up until Terry took his job as Sheriff, he'd spent every other Saturday helping the old man with everything from mowing the yard to re-roofing the house. Now, time and cancer had finally taken Wiggins out of the Hell this world was becoming and Terry owed it to the old man to see that he didn't come back.

Mrs. Wiggins was already waiting for Terry on the porch as he made his way across the yard. Her wrinkled face was full of heartbreak mingling with fear. Her watery eyes looked at him, pleading, as she spoke. "I tied him up Terry. Just like we're supposed to when someone dies. He's locked in the bedroom upstairs."

Terry moved to get by her, heading into the house through the unlocked screen door, as she laid a hand on his shoulder and stopped him. "Terry," she said in a trembling voice, "He was a good man. Do you really think he'll come back?"

Terry averted his eyes from her face and didn't answer. *Everyone came back.* He pulled the .38 from the holster on his belt and checked its chamber then went on into the house.

Even as he reached the bottom of the stairs which led up to the bedroom, he could hear the thumping noises coming from the room. He steeled himself and went up. When he opened the door, he saw Wiggins' body bound tightly inside a white bed spread. Ropes held the old man's arms close to his body but he still moved, slamming himself over and over against the side of the bed trying to get free. Terry raised his gun and took aim at where he figured Wiggins' forehead was under the sheet. Later, before the final burial, there would be additional precautions.

Downstairs, Mrs. Wiggins heard the shot echo off the walls of the house. It was her breaking point. Terry found her collapsed in her husband's favorite armchair, looking into space. "I'm sorry, Justine." She turned her face from him and taking the subtle hint, he left quietly. She collapsed into the floor sobbing as Terry came walking down the steps towards her. There were patches of splattered blood on his otherwise spotless uniform. He knelt beside her and took her in his arms as tears ran down his own cheeks. Finally, he stood. "Let me know if you need any help with the arrangements," he offered and then he was gone.

～

Amy sat on Cobble's western shore, watching the sun set over the water. Its reflected light swirling on the waves below. The scene was breathtaking but her mind was not on the water or the beauty around her. Her thoughts centered on her father. He had been under such a strain since the "plague" began and now things she knew were worse. His duties were mounting instead of staying manageable as she had hoped, mostly with the arrival of the soldiers. He had started drinking again. She'd found the bottles while cleaning his bedroom. Same hiding places he'd used when her mother had died—vodka, gin. If something didn't change and soon, she wondered how much longer he could hold it together and how long Cobble would last without him. The in-fighting had grown worse when you would think people would unite in common cause—in a sense they were being invaded, however peaceably.

Amy picked up a rock and hurled it in frustration out into the water. It struck the surface with a heavy plunking sound and sunk.

"Not very good at skipping rocks are you?" a voice from behind her asked.

She leapt to her feet, ready to fight or run, turning to see a young man in a military uniform standing behind her. Her startled expression apparently caught him off guard. The smile on his face fell away into a look of regret.

"Hey, I'm sorry. I didn't mean to scare you." He turned to leave.

Amy stammered, ashamed of herself. "Wait. You're with the soldiers aren't you?"

He laughed, looking down at his uniform. "What gave you that idea?"

His face was beautiful, open, with the kindest blue eyes she was sure she'd ever seen. Amy found herself relaxing. "Let's start over, ok?" She extended her hand.

"My name is Amy Madison. I bet you have met my Dad already. He's the sheriff here."

The young man took her hand. "Michael. Around here you'll hear me called 'Drake'. And I haven't had the privilege of actually meeting your father, but I've seen him from a distance."

"Then Drake it is then."

He released her hand and stepped back. "Your father's quite a man from what I have seen so far. You must be very proud of him. From what I have heard, he was responsible for this island not ending up like where I came from."

Amy frowned. "I guess that's true."

Then her expression lightened as she changed the subject. "Where are you from Mr. Drake?"

"Oh, here and there, mostly. When the plague started I was stationed in Texas with Captain Simon. And, please, drop the Mr., it's just Drake."

"He's the guy in charge of your unit?" Amy asked, feeling like an idiot and hoping she was using the correct army jargon.

"Yeah," Drake answered, "He's a good guy most of the time. Our unit had been assigned to protect the N.A.S.A. and C.D.C. labs out west after the plague hit the mainland and the rioting started up. I won't say it was an easy job but we got by okay."

"Texas? Didn't they nuke some big cities in Texas before the government collapsed?"

"Well, they nuked just about all the big cities, New York, Dallas, Houston, and Washington D.C. so not just in Texas. But the government didn't really collapse. They just lost control of things. Last I heard the President was still alive in a bunker somewhere and giving out orders but then that was just a rumor." Drake looked around as the sun final disappeared beneath the waves. "It's beautiful here."

Amy laughed. "I bet so after all the stuff you must have seen."

Drake nodded but didn't answer. Instead he stared up at the stars. "It's funny. One of the first questions most people ask when they meet a soldier like me is whether or not I've killed anyone. You didn't."

Amy grinned. "My Dad's the sheriff, remember? We didn't exactly have it easy here on the island either when the world started falling apart."

Drake looked at her. She was in her own way as breathtaking as the sunset. There was such life in her and hope and innocence. It showed in her eyes as green as the ocean depths.

She noticed his gaze and turned her back to him. "So will you be coming into the town?"

"Yes. I have no doubt of that. It's a small island and we are all going to have to learn how to work together and get along."

"You have very honest eyes."

Drake blinked at Amy's seemingly out of place compliment. His smile was shy, awkward. "Thanks."

"It's late. Dad will be worried." Amy said abruptly, picking up the towel she had been resting on earlier and dusting it off. Her own cheeks had turned a deeper shade of red. "Maybe I'll see you again then."

"I'd like that very much," Drake called after her as headed off in the direction of the town. For the first time in a long while, Lieutenant Michael Drake felt something that had been missing in life. It was an odd feeling and one he could only label "hope".

ᔕᔐ

Markham Road ran along the western beaches of the island. Even before the plague, the western shore was not a highly traveled area. The shores of the western side were mostly rocky cliffs which dropped off sharply to the crashing waves below. There was little to see on this side of the island as it was far from the town of Cobble proper and the ground was not as conducive to growing as the interior itself. There were a few scattered ruins of buildings buried within the western woods from by-gone times of the island, long out grown and forgotten. Yet, even this part of the island needed watching. Tonight it was Deputy Gordon's turn to drive these back winding roadways and keep a look out for any sign of trouble or intruders to the island. He almost laughed to himself at the silliness of it. Didn't the island have enough intruders already?

Not far down the road from where Gordon drove slowly along scanning his searchlight through the darkness, a man walked the dirt road. His skin was as pale as snow though he wore all black. Dark rimmed glasses covered his eyes and reflected the light of the stars above. He was a stranger to Cobble but unlike the masses which had fled the mainland seeking safety and shelter here, he had come for a very different reason. In his long walk across the waves, like Jesus in the storm, he had much time to ponder the enigma of the island. His plan had worked so well everywhere and yet here, for some reason, he had failed in his design. As he heard the approaching car and watched its headlights cut the night, he turned to meet it.

Gordon had been eying the brush surrounding the road so intensely that when he looked up at the road ahead, he'd nearly lost of control of the car and wet himself when he saw the man standing in the vehicle's path. "Jesus!" he yelled, flooring the brakes. The patrol car's wheels slid in the gravel lurching to a halt inches from where the man stood.

The man seemed oddly unmoved by the fact that Gordon had nearly run him over.

Gordon flung his door open and leapt out drawing his .38. "Freeze!" he yelled at the top of his lungs, not really knowing how to handle the situation he'd found himself in.

The man complied. He stared at Gordon through his glasses or at least Gordon thought he could feel the man's eyes cutting into him. He couldn't see through the starlight-filled glass of the man's shades.

"Deputy Gordon, I presume, a pleasure to meet you."

"How the Hell do you know my name?" Gordon asked, taking a step closer and trying to get a better look at the man. He held his .38 outstretched and aimed at the man's heart.

The man raised his hand and pointed at Gordon's

own chest. "Your badge," he answered, smirking at Gordon's apparent unease.

"Shit," Gordon whispered again. "You must have incredible eyes to see it from over there."

"I am sorry for disturbing you, Deputy Gordan, but I was hoping you could direct me to the town of Cobble."

Gordon looked around and then back at the man. "Just where the Hell did you come from buddy? Are you with the army? What the Hell are you doin' way out here?"

"One question at a time, please, sir." The man laughed openly now.

"Where did you come from?" Gordon asked again, motioning his gun at the man.

"That's a rather difficult one to answer. How about we start with your second one instead? No, I am not with the "army", if you can call them that."

"Then where did you come from? You sure as Hell aren't from around here."

"Ah, now you're learning to play...One at a time, one at a time." The man smiled and took a step towards Gordon.

"Which way is Cobble?" the man asked, his voice growing a bit tighter, as he took another step forward.

"Back off," Gordon ordered. "I mean it."

"I am sure you do, sir. But I am a bit pressed for time you see. I've been waiting a very long time and I am growing weary."

The man continued towards Gordon. Gordon's eyes grew wide when the man didn't stop even as he ordered him to a second time. Gordon hated to do it but he pulled the trigger. The .38 rocked in his hands and the shot sang in the wind.

The bullet struck the man dead on. He staggered a step looking as if he might fall to his knees but then he regained his composure and looked up at Gordon.

"Why, Gordon, I didn't think you had it in you."

Gordon blinked and shook his head as if to clear it but the man still stood in front of him, walking towards him. "Oh, Jesus," he muttered and pulled the trigger again. This time the man simply side stepped the bullet in its flight and threw himself towards the deputy. His left hand found the gun in Gordon's grasp and crushed it like paper into a useless wad of metal. His right lifted Gordon into the air effortlessly.

Gordon fought against his hold, his feet kicking in the air, but the stranger merely looked up into Gordon's fear filled eyes and sighed. "It would have been easier if you had just told me you know, perhaps even offered me a ride? Why do you fools always make it so hard on yourselves?"

The man took off his glasses with his free hand and two orbs of burning flames blazed up at Gordon who couldn't help but stare into them. Gordon felt as if he was being pulled into those flames as if falling into some kind of dark, black pit. Gordon's screams echoed in the night.

꙰꙰

Marta Kowanski stared out the kitchen window into the huge back yard and the distant wooden fencing. The two new comers were fitting in with the rest of the children in relative ease. A week since their arrival, Ingrid and Isaac were now not so emaciated. Their clothes and hair were clean; their demeanor, more childlike and care-free than on the morning Jared had brought them over: wild-eyed and cotton-pale, like wraiths, with that shock of red hair the only thing that looked alive about them.

Poor babies, thought Marta. To lose everything—their father right before their very eyes, their mother to the plague, their home. When Jared had brought Ingrid and Isaac he'd told her the circumstances. She'd been appalled, quiet, but secretly she hoped that scoundrel, Shannon, would get his in the end. She never had much cared for that excuse of a human being. She remembered Shannon as a child; even then he was not much for conscience or remorse: picking fights and shooting the beautiful birds out of her trees.

Outside, the children were playing hide-and-go-seek. Isaac trying to keep up with his sister's longer legs, running with his thumb stuck in his mouth, bare-chested and bare-footed, and only his patch-and-cut-off shorts covering his lower body. Isaac followed Ingrid around endlessly, still his lifeline, and he refused to let the girl out of his sight. It was true that children were more resilient than adults, but her children had a long way to overcome the trauma that would probably manifest itself later as they became adolescents. Marta's family had grown to twelve children with the inclusion of Ingrid and Isaac, dependent on the whims of the townsfolk for food and clothing. Terry collected what he could, made sure that the farmers remembered their promise to give produce and what meat could be spared to the orphanage.

Two more children to care for, to feed and clothe. The town folk weren't too happy about providing for two extra bodies. They'd complained about the last child she'd taken in too. Marta felt their resentment more and more lately: in the bruised fruit and vegetables she received, the ragged clothing that wasn't much better than nothing at all; and the meat that grew smaller and smaller in portions...

Caleb, the oldest of her children, had just turned fifteen. She wondered when one of the farmers would come by and make good on the promise she'd given five years back. Ben Tucker had been eyeing Caleb's strong arms last time they'd gone into town, imagining him a good field worker no doubt. And one morning, if not Ben, some other farmer would come by and pick Caleb up and not return him until dusk or later, no time for school or learning a trade besides back-breaking farming, no time for churchgoing during harvest when work would continue almost around the clock.

Marta pressed her palm against her forehead. All she could do was help them survive; feed and shelter them as babies and children, beyond those green years they were at the town's mercy. Was she raising slaves without a voice to their future? No, indentured servants, she admonished herself. *Call it like it is.* The farmers saw it as an investment. And wasn't that better than execution? Than starving to death? Wasn't it the very best she could do with what she had? Wasn't it?

Caleb walked through the door with his arms full of firewood, placed it in the bin beside the fireplace and

smiled tenderly at Marta. "We'll be warm and snug tonight."

And Marta returned the smile best she could. "Thank
you, Caleb. What would I do without you?"

Caleb heard something in her voice. He tilted his head,
sun-streaked hair overly long and shaggy. The smile melted
in degrees from his face. "Mom? Something wrong?"

Marta's lips quivered, he was the first to call her 'mom';
he was the one that always set an example for the rest of
the children. She steeled herself against the mountain of
anguish that was building around her heart. "No Caleb,
just watching Ingrid and Isaac getting along."

Caleb's smile returned. "They're doin' great. I whittled
Isaac an airplane this morning. Got to sandpaper it a little
bit—so he won't get any splinters. He'll like that," he paused
a second and then went on. "Guess Ingrid might like me
to fashion a doll for her when I get a chance."

Marta turned back to the window and the playing children. "That would be so good of you, Caleb. Thank you."

"Got to go meet Terry at the end of the driveway.
Today's drop-off day. Remember?"

"Oh, yes. The rice Carl Porter's sending to us. Be sure
to tell Terry I said thank you."

"We all thank him," Caleb said as he walked to the
door. He stopped in the doorway, squinting out to the end
of the dirt road. "Looks like Terry's not alone today. I think
that's Ben Tucker's pick-up behind him. Wonder what he
wants?"

≈≈

Shannon leaned forward, looking out toward
Halsbrook field. Twenty feet in the air, prostrate, and too
far up for Shannon to be shaky while he balanced his
body on the thick branch and the binoculars on his face;
but didn't he have a bird's eye view: the tents and tin buildings that had gone up overnight, the makeshift shower
stalls that were unisex—and his binoculars locked in that
direction to see the leggy lieutenant smoothing back her
wet hair, face upturned to the water as it rained down and
down where he could only imagine. He cursed; the five

extra feet he'd climbed gave him no better view. He looked around the perimeter for a tree that would grant him better access, but soon gave up on that idea. By the time he climbed down and shimmied up another tree, the show would be over.

Shannon was about to climb down and admit defeat for the day when he heard footsteps through the brush. He pressed himself to the limb and waited, hoping that he couldn't be seen.

Two men walked the path and halted beneath him. If he slipped—if he fell from the tree, he would land on top of them—game over. His heart thudded in his chest and he tried to slow his breathing. The tall man—graying white at the temples, gait rhythmic and assured—he recognized as Captain Simon. The other shorter man was the doctor, the scientist that thought he knew how to cure the plague with the help of their little island. Shannon doubted there was anything on the island that could stop the plague, but then he wasn't a man of science. His education was limited and filled with holes from cutting class and scribbling comic strips instead of algebra equations. It just seemed to him a waste of time to be looking for a cure here; the plague didn't start here. It wasn't like they had grown some new kind of antibiotic or made a new wonder drug, or discovered a new plant. They didn't even have a hospital, barely had a doctor.

The captain's eyes panned around them and satisfied they were alone, crossed his arms. "Safe enough to talk here. Not that I don't trust my men, just never can be too careful with sensitive information."

"Oh, I quite agree, Captain. The Sheriff may prove to be more difficult than we thought; he wasn't exactly thrilled at our suggestion of child labor. The town must have overruled him; we must have appealed to their capitalist side. They keep working their regular jobs and we turn the children's paycheck over to them. How could we have known they'd have their own child labor system already in place on the island? That information was like gold. All the while we get cheap labor," he smirked as if relishing in an inside joke. "Cheap associates." But then he straightened his lanky frame, all business and rubbing his dry palms together. "I wanted to know what to expect in the coming week. My laboratory was fully functional *yesterday*." He leaned in, almost touched Simon's pointed nose causing Simon to blink, the slightest of jerks in a man of steady discipline. "I'm eager to begin."

Simon's nostrils flared and he regained his dead-eye stare. "The first of the children will arrive early this evening. I'm having them escorted over by our friend and ally, the good doctor of the island himself." A laughless smile intended to flash sharp teeth, to make Paxton pause on the edge of uncomfort, coiled, rigid and tight. "I have a lot invested in you, Paxton. No mistakes this time. No excuses." He turned as to leave the way he came, boots stamping the dried leaves, whirled around to add something and Paxton startled, turned red and clenched his jaw. Simon pressed his advantage, walking into Paxton's personal space, his height advantage more evident in the six inches that separated them. "Oh, one more thing. Leave Lieutenant Hannigan alone. She couldn't possibly further your goals, only hinder them."

And Paxton nearly laughed, had to swallow his enthusiasm before it was detected. *Foolish, foolish man.* Simon had just handed him his four-star Achilles heel on the most delectable of platters.

⁂

Deputy Gordon had called in sick this morning and Terry missed him at his side as he climbed out of his patrol car. Today was not going to be an easy day. He could see Caleb running down Marta's drive to meet him already, excitement on the boy's face. Ben and Carl looked over at Terry grim faced. They knew what Terry was about to ask of Marta and didn't approve, though they had came along to support him in his talk with her if necessary.

Terry knew he had done all he could. When he'd heard of the "deal" Mayor Beck had cut with the island's new arrivals, he'd stormed into the Beck's house and shoved his way past the mayor's wife to his study which passed for his office these days. He had to admit he hadn't handled things in the most delicate fashion but he'd just came from sending one of his closest friends back to Hell. He could still hear Mrs. Wiggins' sobs ringing in his ears. He'd shouted, yelled, even threatened to resign as sheriff but Beck had stood firm. The children would be in no danger, he'd claimed and they *needed* what the unit encamped in Halsbrook field had to offer too badly to refuse.

As Caleb reached them, Terry put on a smile as best he could. "Morning, Caleb. How's Marta today?" he asked.

"She's fine, Sheriff. Do you need help unloading the rice?" He glanced eagerly at Ben's truck and noticed it was empty though Carl was with Ben as usual. Confusion registered in his brown eyes and he looked back at Terry.

"Not today, son. I need to talk to talk to Marta is she in the house?"

"Yes, sir."

"Will you take me to her?"

Caleb nodded and stared back up the drive with Terry and Ben following behind him.

Gordon sat on his couch rubbing at his eyes. He had been throwing up all morning and didn't know why. He couldn't remember much about his patrol of the island the night before but as far as he could remember nothing unusual had happened. The only odd thing he *could* remember was driving out to the old cemetery before coming home. That struck him as odd. His left leg hurt like Hell too. When he'd found the courage to pull up the leg of his pants and look at it, he'd discovered a wound there. It looked as if someone or something had taken a chunk out of lower leg but it was scabbed over already and wasn't bleeding. It merely leaked a sick looking, yellow puss around its sides. How in the Hell could he not remember something like that happening?

A recollection of seeing wounds like it dogged his memory but refused to come into the light. He cursed himself for being so careless last night whatever he had been up to then leapt up from the couch, running for the toilet as a wave of nausea came over him violently once more.

When he was done, he reached up and flushed the bowl with a tired hand. He rested on his knees in the floor struggling not to start heaving again. He knew that there was nothing left inside of him. There couldn't be. As he sat there, he began to remember bits and pieces of the night before as they flashed into his mind like a random slideshow, but none of what he recalled made any sense. It was all like some kind of jumbled and impossible nightmare. He remembered shooting somebody, a man he'd never seen before, only the man hadn't died. It hadn't been a man at all. The thing had sat in the passenger seat of his patrol car looking human all the same. It had ordered him to show it to the cemetery after it...had what? Raped his mind hunting through his thoughts about the island and its people? It just didn't make any sense. The only other thing he recalled was a name, "Cryten", that had seemed to be howled like a curse by the wind of the island itself.

Gordon got to his feet and managed to stagger back to the couch in the living room. He collapsed onto it as his reeling mind spun into darkness and he passed out.

⚬⚬

Christina was arranging the last of the faded-olive blankets over the rattan sofa—crudely made and splintery, but what wasn't in these times—when the knock on the door of the cabin startled her. Ten o'clock, who could that be, she thought, smoothing the corner of the sofa. She didn't unchain the door but opened it to peer through the space the chain allowed.

"Do you have a moment, Lieutenant?" Simon leaned into the door, propping his weight against the door with his arm

"Could it not wait until morning, Captain?" Her hand gripped the door handle tighter as she strained to keep her voice respectful. "I'm not dressed for company at this hour."

Simon straightened, cleared his throat then smiled through the three-inch gap. His eyes seemed to sweep everywhere: into the cabin, trying his best to peek at her from around the door, his gaze traveling down to her bare feet and the pink of her polished toenails. "I'm sorry to disturb you at this hour, but I'm not here on a social call, Christina. Official business does not wait for banker hours; we have to talk."

Her name sounded forced from his mouth, indecent and lewd, with a premeditated feel to it, and why shouldn't it? she thought. It wasn't like he went around calling her by her given name; it was a first, and it made her feel uneasy, not helped by the fact that she stood behind the door vulnerable in her thin pajamas. He could have simply told her what it was that was so darn important through the door instead of making it sound like a polite order, like he was pulling rank—he still in uniform and she in her sleep attire—the nerve of him.

"I see," she replied frostily. "If you'll wait for a moment while I get my robe."

Simon did not wait for a reply, but shut the door firmly. His smug face was as she stalked to the closet and jerked the heavy cotton robe from the wire hanger. She slid her feet into the fuzzy yarn slippers and, in afterthought, grabbed her shower cap from the bathroom shelf. *Must make myself as appealing as possible for the good captain*, she hissed, then smiled as she dipped her fingers into the jar of cold cream on the stand.

She opened the door wide, befitting a king, and even bowed slightly. "Won't you come in?" and the look of the bewildered Captain as he removed his hat and shuffled in, beyond price, beyond mere authority: Beware the female tiger as she looked on through the mask of paste-white cream, feral and cunning, the sweet tang of victory in the stunned air between them.

He sat down on the sofa like a deflated lung, that gruff clearing of his throat the only sound in the room as she sat in the rattan chair across from him.

A few awkward seconds and then he spoke to his hat still clutched in both of his hands. "Well, Lieutenant, like I said, I'm sorry to umm bother you this evening." Another few seconds of silence as the captain rotated the hat around in his hands. "The sheriff is to bring by the first haul of children for you to ready for Dr. Paxton first thing in the morning. Now, what I'd like to do is get you to make sure all the children are physically, well, I mean healthy enough, to assist the doctor. We need to know that these children are mentally stable as well as fit. Paperwork will need to be filled out. The usual preliminary work-up."

"Children? What do you mean by children?"

"The orphanage is where we will be getting Dr. Paxton's *work force*. They'll assist the doctor in his research. We've worked out a little contract with the islanders. Seems they want these kids to start earning their keep."

"Children?"

"Not children, really," he said. His face was flushed. "They'll all be over the age of thirteen."

"*Children*. They're still children at that age."

"Evidently, the islanders don't quite see it that way, Lieutenant." Sweat was starting to bead over his bushy eyebrows.

"Children of that age, under sixteen at least, need to be in school. We are denying them that right!"

"Desperate times, Christina. Please, there will be time for school when all this plague mess is put behind us—"

"I find child labor incredibly distasteful. Even with the plague decimating us as it has we have to retain our values. Surely this is not your idea of civilized society, Captain? Surely not your suggestion…"

Simon puffed up and tore his eyes away from his hands, conceiving a way out of her disfavor. "Oh no, Christina. Not my idea at all." He leaned forward as if taking her into his confidence. "Dr. Paxton masterminded the whole affair, I just went along with it, and as I said, the islanders agreed. I knew this would upset you, moral creature that you are, and I just *had* to come by and inform you of this business myself. This is as distasteful to me as it is to you, but for the good of the whole I'm resigning myself to this temporary solution."

"How long does he want to use the children?"

Simon smiled and rose from the creaking sofa. "A few short months. I'll put an end to it if Paxton doesn't at the end of twelve weeks. I give you my promise, Christina."

She locked the door behind the captain and leaned heavily against it, wiping away the cold cream and wondering just who won the victory after all.

❧

Marta replayed Terry's words over and over in her head but still couldn't come to terms with it. *Her children were to be used as labor and maybe even "lab-rats".* It tore her up inside and made her want to scream but she realized there was nothing she could do. Meeting Terry outside on the steps with her old 12 gauge wasn't an option. She respected Terry and knew he would have done all he could to prevent this abomination. The mayor and his deals, she thought, how could he?

The house was still and quiet. It was long past midnight and all the kids were long tucked into bed. Caleb and Robbie were even excited to be going tomorrow morning. They didn't realize what they were getting into she guessed. Pulling her house coat tighter around her, she moved to the kitchen cabinet and opened it. She took down a battered can of coffee possibly one of the last few left on the island, and went to make herself a cup. It was going to be a long night of worrying and she needed something to get her through.

❧

As the sun rose above Cobble, Dr. Paxton waited eagerly for his new help to arrive as he paced outside his newly set up lab. Privates Bates and Coleman were with him for security but he paid them no mind. He had long gotten used to ignoring Simon's underlings.

Paxton watched as a pick-up truck made its way down the dusty road on the edge of town towards his lab. Its bed was filled with seven youths and as it drew closer he could see the island's doctor and another man inside the cab with a boy sitting between them.

The truck pulled into the drive and stopped as its occupants began to unload themselves from its rusty confines.

A smile stretched across Paxton's face. Everything was

going just as he planned. Soon he would have all he needed to start his work again. He was so close to understanding the nature of the plague and finding a way to stop it. Paxton swore to himself, no matter the cost, this time he would find and isolate the cause of the plague and finish developing his vaccine. Nothing else mattered if the human race as a species was going to have a chance to survive.

᠊ᡐᡐ᠊

Father Ensley knelt on his knees before the statue of Jesus. His eyes were downcast and the whisper of prayers echoed in the vacant church. He prayed for the Lord to grant the sheriff the strength to make it through this new crisis. He had heard the talk of the island giving up its children to the military entrenched in Halsbrook field in trade for supplies and it tore at his heart. Very few people ever came to his sermons anymore. Even before the plague, Cobble was not exactly an island full of devout believers and since the outbreak of the dead, it seemed most of the people here possessed nothing left in their hearts for God but hatred. "How could a loving and forgiving God let this happen to the world?" they argued. Ensley had to admit, he didn't have an answer to that one. Inwardly though, he kept his faith. The Lord did have a plan. He knew that in his heart of hearts even if he didn't understand it. He knew that the churches on the mainland had become death traps during the end days of the plague before humanity was as scattered and as few in numbers as it was today. People had flocked to them looking for safety and turning to God for help as the dead surrounded them and tore at the buildings relentlessly until they gained entrance and enjoyed a feast of believers' flesh.

Pastor Ensley heard the heavy wooden doors of *his* church creak open. He got to his feet and moved to greet the man who walked down the isle towards him. As the man drew closer in the light of the flickering candles of the room, Ensley realized he'd never seen this person before. He was clearly not of the island. His clothes were all black and dark glasses covered the windows to his soul. As Ensley moved to outstretch his hand in greeting, only then did he notice the small whiffs of smoke coming from where the man's feet touched the church's floor, lingering briefly in the air, after each footstep before more were formed.

Ensley jerked his hand back as fear shot through him. He yanked the cross he wore on a necklace under his shirt from around his neck and held it out towards the man.

"There is no place for you," Ensley warned. "Get out of my church and off Cobble."

The man laughed, his voice an eerie sound, like a thousand souls screaming.

"Where is your Christian kindness, Father?" the man grinned. "I have traveled far and grow weary. May I not rest here on my path?"

"In the name of Jesus, hallowed be thy name!!" Ensley began to yell, but the man reached out and bent the pastor's arm awkwardly to the left at an unnatural angle. The pastor howled as tears poured down his cheeks from the pain.

"We'll have none of that, little man," the man said as he caught the pastor's collapsing form and pulled him close against his body, hugging the pastor's head. With a simple twist, he snapped Ensley's neck before letting the holy man drop the rest of the way to the floor.

"I just need to kill a bit of time here, priest. Then I'll get out of your way," the man said to Ensley's corpse. He sat down on the closest bench as smoke rose in waves around him. "It won't be too long now." His laughter shattered the stain glass windows around him, as the glass clinked to rest on the wood below like rain.

⚜

Deputy Gordon Hughes sat on his couch, unmoving, with a puke and blood stained blanket resting over his body. It was pulled nearly up to his chin. He had been so cold before the seizures had come and his heart had stopped beating inside his chest. His film-covered eyes stared hollowly at the ceiling above him. He knew somehow through the fog of his mind that he died, but he could still think somehow. Slowly, he stumbled to his feet, the blanket dropping off him. The pain from his wounded leg had stopped troubling him and the cold had faded. Now, he felt nothing. His thoughts drifted to Terry. Would Terry understand he was still Gordon or would the sheriff put a bullet into his skull when they next met? He and Terry had been friends forever. Surely, Terry wouldn't simply gun him down like...like the thing he had become.

Gordon stiffly bent over and reached for his gun which lay on the coffee table in front of the couch and tried to slip it into the holster on his belt like he did every morning before work. His movements were clumsy and it took a few attempts before he had it in place but when he did, he nodded to himself and headed for the door. It was time to go back to work.

ॐॐ

Christina hadn't slept well after Simon's visit. The morning was here now and there was nothing for it. She made her way across her quarters while she finished pulling on her uniform. It was going to be a busy day and she was already late. She glanced at her watch, thankful its battery still worked. She was an hour behind and Paxton would have a field day with it. The Doctor would hold it over her head for the rest of the day. It *was* very unlike her. She hated Simon standing by and allowing the doctor to test his vaccine on the children under the guise of using them as laborers. She had no doubt *that* was his real intention. She replayed Simon's words in her head. "I'll put an end to it if the doctor doesn't at the end of twelve weeks," he said. What he had meant was that if the doc didn't have results on a workable vaccine or cure in that amount of time, the doc wouldn't be a part of the unit anymore. Paxton would find himself drifting on the oceans waves as fish food with a hole from a 9mm round in his forehead. She'd seen Simon do the like before, even done it for him, but for some reason now, it felt like time was running out and judgment was coming.

She picked up her M-16 rifle and checked its clip. This time things would be different when Simon started up his old tricks. She didn't need him anymore. She could live here on Cobble without the bloodshed and horrors of the mainland following. She could at least after Simon was dead. Seeing that the gun was loaded and in working order, she walked outside into the light of the sun.

❦

For the first time in weeks, since before Simon and his cohorts had arrived, Terry decided to walk to the station. It wasn't far and it let him see how the town folks were getting along. A slow walk instead of driving past might even give them a sense of normalcy, calm their minds. Terry left the cottage and took the narrow path that would emerge onto the dirt road. It was a shortcut through heavy forest for a quarter of a mile but then it would end right beside the church and the Tompkins's home, where the official township began and continued for two blocks. Not a large town by any means, but they got along. He saw to it that they got along fine—without outside help.

Terry moved down the footpath leisurely. The path had always seemed peaceful to him and this part of his walk he always slowed for: the tropical birds overhead with their squawks, hedgehogs chattering and darting in and out of the pathway, sometimes right over his feet. The buzz of insects in the air, and large patches of foliage blooming fist-sized white and pink flowers, trailing vines and a shiny wet dew on the dark green leaves. There was something about nature that could heal past wounds, and maybe that was why the island was such an ideal place for them, maybe that's why the ruin of the rest of the world seemed so remote. That was also why Simon and Paxton sought the island out too, he supposed, if Paxton could be believed when he claimed he needed the island's diverse and lush plant life.

There was a small clearing ahead and Terry paused. He thought he heard something rustle the in the dense shrubbery and trees. For a moment or two he stood perfectly still and quiet, almost dismissing the sound as birds playing, but then he heard it again, louder.

He crept up the path and then left it altogether, weaving and pushing through the vines and brambles, trying to be as silent as possible.

And then to his left, something moved. Lightning fast. Inhumanly fast. Terry tried to follow the sound it was making, taking up chase through the uneven terrain, briars pricking and tearing his skin and clothes, and still he couldn't get close enough to the dark figure to see any details. It was a human shape; at least he had thought so when he caught it out of the corner of his eye, initially. But people don't move that fast, he thought to himself. No one can move that fast. And he found himself questioning whether he saw a human or not. Maybe just a distorted shadow, the sun was slanting in through the trees...

Huffing and leaning against one of the tall trees, Terry gave up the pursuit. Whatever it was, it was gone now, vanished into the forest and at such a distance away that Terry couldn't hear its movements or see its departure. Could an animal move that fast? He should have at least been able to see its flight through the woods as he pursued it. And why did he pursue it? If it was just an animal...why? He didn't really believe it to be an animal, not in the cute furry sense of the word. Human animal, that had been his instinct, his gut reaction to the shadowy presence. But would he ever be sure...and why did it bother him so?

He stood there regaining his breath and listening for a moment longer, then made his way back to the foot path, his mind still turning over the events. His analytical mind tried to make sense of it all but there was no rationale. The more his head cleared, the more the pursuit felt like a game...the figure had known Terry couldn't catch it, not with that speed...

Terry was coming up on the spot where he'd first seen the shadowy phantom—and phantom was just what he was going to call it if he couldn't put a more definitive name to it—the sun's rays were now streaming behind him, and from this direction he could see something glinting on the ground where the noise had first caught his attention.

Terry walked over to the spot hoping that it was some

sort of clue to the phantom's identity. Looking down at the spot, it appeared to be a heap of clothing. Reaching down he tugged at a corner of black shiny material. The cloth reminded him of something. He tugged but the cloth seemed to be caught on something on the ground. He tugged harder and the cloth ripped through, revealing what lie beneath. *Jesus.* He stumbled backwards falling hard against the trees, the air knocked from his lungs long before the impact. It was Father Ensley, or what was left of him. The splintered bones had knotted and stitched the wet black robe together. The old pastor's seminary ring—the only thing that identified him as Ensley—still glinted in the morning sun on what used to be a hand, but now resembled the rest of the pulverized and twisted body. He'd never in all his law enforcement days seen anything like it.

Terry struggled to his feet and took to running down the path. He no longer thought of the fleeing figure as a phantom. What they had on the island was much worse than a phantom or even the undead the plague had brought. What they had was something more hideous and dangerous than anything man could physically become. They had a monster on the loose.

❧

Jared sat across the room from Dr. Paxton who had reclined comfortably into the chair of his new office. Both men stared at one another trying to hide the contempt they felt. "Coffee? I am afraid military issue is all I have to offer, but it does the job just the same," Paxton offered, motioning to a thermos sitting before him on his desk.

"No thanks," Jared waved the offer aside, "I didn't come here to drink coffee." Jared glanced out the window of the office at the driveway where the children were still at work unloading a new batch of chemicals and the like, just as Simon had cut a deal with the island for. Most of it came from Jared's own supply. He felt anger at that fact and was forced to remind himself why he *was* here.

"While I thank you, Doctor Jones, for delivering the children I am rather pressed for time. So why don't you say whatever it is you feel you must and let's get on with our lives."

Paxton was a quite few years younger than Jared and filled with an arrogance that grated on Jared's nerves. Paxton was a researcher, not a real doctor in the sense that he was, and he hated leaving the children to be attended by this man. "Why do you even need our children, Paxton? Can't your captain's grunts do the work these kids are doing?"

Paxton laughed loudly, leaning across his desk to look closer at Jared. "Captain Simon and I don't always see eye to eye. He has his own uses for his men, I guess, that keep them from being here as more than guards. I am just a doctor trying to save the world, what do I know about military procedures and practices?"

It was Jared's turn to eye Paxton. "If I even suspect that your uses for the children are for anything more than labor and the like, I will kill you, sir."

Paxton sighed. "This isn't the school yard, doctor. Aren't you a little old to be making threats?" Paxton turned towards the window. "Private Thompson! Come and show our good doctor the way out please."

Jared's cheeks flushed with anger as the soldier entered the room. Thompson carried an AK-47 rifle and Jared could tell from the look on the man's face that the safety was off.

Jared rose from his seat. "We'll speak again, Paxton. You can count on it."

"Oh, how much I will be looking forward to that, Dr. Jones," Paxton grinned.

Thompson stepped aside so Jared could leave the room first and followed him out.

Paxton shuffled a stack of papers on his desk, his confrontation with Jared forgotten and shoved to the back of his mind even as the door to his office closed. He glanced out the window himself, one thought in his mind. "Where the Hell is Christina?" he muttered to himself. It was very unlike her to be late.

⤳⤳

Terry stood watching Simon stare down in disbelief at the corpse-thing that had been the island's Priest which lay at his feet. Mayor Beck waited behind them, wiping sweat from his wrinkled brow with a white cloth. Three of Simon's soldiers, all armed to the teeth, along with Shannon and Ben Tucker, who carried only powerful hunting rifles, prowled the woods around them, alert and on edge.

"Well sheriff, this certainly isn't work of the reanimates as we have come to know them. It would take something far stronger than even a pack of them to mangle a man like that. Look at the corpse, it's too messed up to become one of those things, but there doesn't look to be any teeth marks or bites on it anywhere. If it had been the undead, they would have surely fed on it some."

"I know that," Terry growled in frustration. "I want to know what the Hell did do this and I want to know now."

"I assure you, I would tell you if I knew, Terry. May I call you, Terry?"

The sheriff nodded.

"Can we please show a little respect here, gentlemen, and cover his body at least?" Mayor Beck asked, looking on the verge of being sick.

Both Terry and Simon turned to look at the elderly man.

"I think we should take the body back to Paxton's new lab in town. Let him run some tests. He may be able to shed some light on this mess," Simon suggested.

"Don't either of you realize what this means?" Terry strained to hold his temper. "We've got something or someone on this island who's killed at least one person already. What if his next victim is in better shape? Did you think of that? They'd get up and then we'd have two killers to deal with. This could get out of hand overnight. We have to do something more than just sit around playing detective."

"And what would you have us do?" Simon asked. "My unit has traveled across the whole of the US since the plague started before ending up here and I have never seen anything like this. Are we to assemble a mob and go about beating the bushes? Wouldn't that in its self start a panic that could be just as disastrous?" Simon aimed his last question at the Mayor not Terry.

"The captain's right, Terry. We can't let word of this get out yet. Folk here are under enough stress already. I don't want someone getting the wrong idea and going after our new friends." Mayor Beck nodded at Simon and his men.

"This is a small island," Terry shot back, "Most people will know about this before supper time, whatever we do."

"My men won't be the source if they do, Sheriff," Simon smiled. He turned and started shouting orders. "Get this body loaded up. I want it over to Paxton's ASAP. Keep it under cover."

As Simon swaggered over to watch the body being loaded, Terry moved closer to Beck. "Look, I put up with your selling our children off like slaves but I am not going to allow you to risk all that we have worked and bled for here. I'm going to find out who did this tonight and I don't give a damn who knows it."

"Terry," Beck started in a warning tone before noticing the looks of Ben Tucker and Shannon behind the sheriff. Their faces were hard and Shannon snapped a round into the chamber of his .30-.06. Beck sighed. "Fine, have it your way, Terry. But you had better keep things under control. Simon and his men had nothing to do with this."

"I'm glad you're so sure," Terry said sarcastically as he turned away and headed for his car.

❧❧

Christina pushed the flap back to enter Paxton's tent. His makeshift laboratories encompassed 7 of the larger tents. Prime tents, sturdier than what the rest of them had though still smaller than his lab in town that the islanders had allowed him to set up to make due with, except for her, she had obtained one of the two cabins in the field. Paxton also had his lab in town set up in house that the islanders had loaned him but these tents had been where he had first set up and he still worked here from time to time. Terry had told her that her own cabin used to be an old hunting cabin. Paxton turned, glared at her then pointedly looked at his watch.

"Yes, I realize I'm late and that I never made it your other lab. Couldn't be helped; Marta came by this morning as I was leaving." Hands on her hips now, as she glared back at Paxton. "She's really upset about the kids, you know."

Paxton bent and picked up a large crate and placed it on the table between them. "Of course she's upset. Old Mother Hubbard is finding her shoe empty, Lt. Hannigan. I…I mean, we, need the children a little more than she does. For the sake of all humankind." He opened the crate and began rummaging around. "Some sacrifices must be made."

"Certainly, *Doctor*," she said with a bite of sarcasm.

Paxton abruptly stopped his search through the crate, looked up and sighed.

"Lt. Hannigan, please. We have much bigger problems this morning. Much bigger—"

"What do you mean?"

"Details are sketchy at the moment, but we may have another epidemic here on the island. Seems the local priest has been murdered. Oh no, not merely murdered, brutalized. It would have to be truly horrific for our captain to lack an accurate description and grow pale at the mention of it."

"Here?"

Paxton nodded. "The captain will brief you on the situation when he returns," he looked at his watch again, "which should be any minute now."

Christina put her hand to her forehead. "This is horrible."

"This is why we're here, Lt. Hannigan, to rid the world of this scourge. Please, won't you become part of the solution…forget your societal differences until we can make some progress? We're all working under stressful conditions—the whole world is one big stressful condition."

"Where are the pastor's remains?"

"With Drake for the time being. His previous work in forensics is making him quite useful to us. But I warn you, Lt. Hannigan, I've been told it isn't a pretty sight."

Christina made for the exit. "It never is as far as the plague is concerned. Thank you for the warning, though."

Outside, she walked westward to the group of tents where she knew she'd find Drake. At the very least, she would get straight honest answers from him. No one was willing to give Drake his due except when they needed something from him: his expertise, his multi-linguistics... But there was something else about Drake—something she couldn't quite put her finger on. The man had integrity, but that wasn't exactly it either. It was something indiscernible; a feeling, really. Maybe just her woman's intuition, the men just skimmed over it. Or maybe it was just her own imagination. Not the honesty of the man, no, she'd bet the farm on his character, but that which was hidden further underneath. And Christina laughed out loud, laughed at herself for such odd thoughts; she sounded like some spiritual advisor. All she needed was a crystal ball and some tea leaves. Yeah, well, she thought, stranger things had been known to happen—take the plague for instance. She picked up her pace, suddenly impatient to talk to Drake and find out what he thought of the recent events. Good ole' shoot-from-the-hip Drake. What a pleasant change in atmosphere that would be.

≈≈

Terry's patrol car pulled into the drive in front of Gordon's house. Ben Tucker rode in the passenger seat while Shannon sat in the back. The three men got out and headed for the house. Gordon had missed work for the second day in a row and this time hadn't even bothered to call in. Terry was more than a little worried about his friend and deputy. It was a custom on Cobble to visit the sick. It was something that had to be done, regardless of who it was or what they may have because if that person died, someone had to know about it and take the necessary steps. Terry was haunted by memories of Wiggins which still burned freshly in his mind. He prayed he wouldn't be forced to "put down" another friend so soon.

The three men made their way up to the front door. There was no answer to their knocking or Shannon's irate yells. Finally, Terry tried the knob. The door was open and the men let themselves inside.

The living room was a mess. Bottles of various medicines littered the top of the coffee table in front of the couch and an uneaten plate of food that looked to be over a day old sat molding beside them. The couch itself was smeared with dried blood and a stained blanket rested on the floor near it. Patches of bloody vomit trailed away from the couch leading into Gordon's bathroom but there was no sign of the deputy from where they stood.

"Jesus, it stinks in here," Shannon said, making his way to the kitchen without looking back.

Ben walked over and checked the bedroom, moving deeper inside to check the bath as well. When Ben stepped into the bath, he was forced to cover his nose and mouth with his hand. The stench of sickness and decay that filled the room was stronger than anywhere else in the house and so strong it nearly made Ben gag and be sick himself. The toilet bowl was full of blood and the carpet stained a dark red all across the room. Ben noticed that the bath's mirror had been shattered as if someone had struck it with a bare handed blow. He stepped back out of the room, closing the door behind him and turned as he called to Terry, "He's not here!"

As Terry knelt to pick up the blanket, Shannon came out of the kitchen holding a beer, struggling to unscrew the bottle's top. "He's dead, Sheriff. There ain't no doubt about it."

Terry's eyes were filled with anger as he watched Shannon get the cap off and down a good portion of the beer. Shannon smiled, "He's a walker now."

Terry leapt up lunging at Shannon. He caught the burly man off guard and slammed him hard into the wall, pinning him there. Shannon's beer fell to the floor and rolled away, its contents emptying into the carpet. Shannon fought against Terry's grip which grew tighter about his neck. "What the Hell's wrong with you?" He managed, in a choked voice.

"You will show some respect," Terry warned. "Gordon was ten times the man you'll ever be."

"Terry, let him go," Ben ordered, pointing his rifle at the sheriff. "He isn't worth it."

Terry released his hold and backed off. Shannon rubbed at the red skin of his throat, hatred boiling out of him. "Fuck both of you!" Shannon raged. "It's time we had someone in charge on this island who doesn't have his head up his ass. That Captain Simon at least seems to know how to get things done. He'll find Gordon and when he does, he won't take this crap. He'll do what needs doin' and won't give it a second thought."

Shannon stormed out of Gordon's home, slamming the front door behind him.

"He's right about one thing, Terry," Ben stated. "We're going to have to find Gordon and take care of him. One way or another."

"I know," Terry nodded, "I know. But why did it have to happen now in the middle of all this?"

Ben laid a hand on Terry's shoulder. "The Lord works in mysterious ways, my friend. We've just got to have faith that he has a plan."

Terry pulled away. He wiped at his eyes with the back of his hand and fished his car keys out his pocket. "We need to get going. We're going to need some more help if we're going to find Gordon and whatever killed the priest too. And I think I know where we can find it but first we have an errand to run."

꿈꿈

Shannon watched the patrol car pull away from his hiding place in the bushes around Gordon's house. That shit-head of a sheriff had bitten off more than he could chew this time. Shannon shook his head and wondered how the asshole would die. Would he find Gordon first and let his "friend" tear him a new one or would the captain finally get as sick of the bastard as he was and put a bullet in his brainpan? He didn't suppose it mattered. If all else failed, he'd take Terry out himself. He'd wanted to for years, dreamed of taking a 12 gauge at point blank and having a go at Terry's stomach, watching the man's intestines fall out of the wound and dangle on the ground as he bled to death begging for help. Shannon laughed at the image, just as in his dreams he laughed at Terry's pleading face as the sheriff "bled out", slowly and painfully. It made him warm and fuzzy inside. Still grinning, he got up from where he squatted and started back into Gordon's home.

There was more beer to be had. Sure it was island brew, but it was free, and he knew Gordon had been a gun freak too. It was time to check out the deputy's collection. Gordon wouldn't be needin' them now anyway.

As Shannon came back out he heard a twig snap beside of him from the bushes. It startled him and he whirled around and jerked up his .30-06 as a gunshot rang out in the night. Shannon's eyes focused on Gordon. A confused look spread across Shannon's features, as he felt the warm red liquid trickle down his face from the hole that had appeared in his forehead. Then Shannon toppled to the ground in front of the corpse. Gordon slowly lowered his smoking .38, his cracked lips moving as he tried to speak. "Fffffuuukkkgggguuuuu," Gordon moaned. The .38 slid out his rotting hands but he didn't even seem to notice. What little of his mind had remained his transformation was changing. In the history of the plague, no one had ever changed like him. Most zombies were mindless from the get-go. He was thankful he'd had a bit more time of being able to think before the hunger took him but now something pulled at his mind. It was like sinking in a lake of black water. Something was happening to him beyond death and rising up as one of the creatures he'd killed so many of. Someone or something seemed to exist inside his mind with him. He moaned again and began to lumber down the road in the direction Terry had driven, his wounded leg dragging on the pavement.

The lighting was bad inside the tent, dim and not much better than having a few candles. When Christina pulled the flap back and called "Hello?" the sunlight poured in causing Drake to shield his eyes in her direction. He sat at a small laminated table, pen in hand, his bold longhand scribble on the notepad in front of him and quickly he closed it.

"Come in," he called; his smooth voice was a polite tenor as he folded his hands with the pen still caught between his fingers.

"Hope I'm not interrupting—"

"No, no, Lt. Hannigan," he said, "please, come in." Drake strode to the corner of the tent and retrieved a folding chair for her, pushed the seat down and indicated for her to have a seat. She took the seat, "thank you."

"Paxton said that you had the remains of the priest. Have you found anything yet? I mean...is it the plague?

A long pause lingered in the air while Drake weighed his words carefully. "Not the plague in the sense of what we've dealt with in the past."

"A new strain, then?" her stomach tightened; her fingers went rigid on the surface of the table, gripping the smooth surface.

Drake stared at the cover of the notebook he'd just written in. She wondered what revelations his notes contained; she was certain he wouldn't share all his findings with her. But what of Paxton and Simon, did he plan on disclosing all his data to them?

Did he have a choice? Or did Paxton already know what Drake had found?

Drake stood, turned his back to her and walked to the far side of the tent where another table was crowded against the tent wall: aluminum tray covered with a slicker-like coverlet, microscope, and several small containers. The aluminum tray would contain the remains.

"I'm afraid it's more complicated than just another strain of the plague. Plague isn't the term I myself would use..."

"What are you saying?" she asked, wanting to understand, but did she really want to know? Christina was alarmed at the gravity in the man's face; this was something infinitely worse than their wildest nightmares—what she considered the plague to be. What could be worse than the plague? She willed her body to stay seated when every cell in her body screamed for her to get up and run,

run until there was no breath left.

"Do you trust Paxton?"

And what kind of question was that—laying such a question at her feet. She could have him cancelled for the mere implication of it. He knew this, which meant only one thing to her: Drake trusted her. He was laying much more than a simple question at her feet, he was laying down his life. Under normal circumstances it would be preposterous, foolish; she would expect some sort of set up, a recording device to railroad or blackmail. But with Drake she didn't even entertain the possibility. He was above those tactics and she knew this to be the truth, knew it from deep down where there was no source of proof, just conviction. She shook her head, *no, no; I don't trust either of them; I didn't think I trusted anyone*, still shaking her head in disbelief. *No. No*; in relief: capable of trusting once again. She'd lost that part of herself so long ago. Trust. With her life, *yes; yes.*

"Do you want to see?"

It took her a moment to realize he was talking of the remains, that he had already uncovered the deep aluminum tray. He was standing in front of it, the only barrier to her eyes. Say the word and it's yours; your nightmare, your problem to share...with this man: 'til death do you part...

She pushed up from the table with her hands, the faint imprint of moisture on the surface, brief tattoo of her soul already fading at the edges. Lightheaded, with legs full of quiver, she closed the space between them, stood at his side, her accomplice in whatever may come, still not looking at the contents of the tray. Not yet; not yet.

Drake's low-throated voice, almost a sigh, "This wasn't done by man."

She slowly turned her head to the tray, to the monstrosity, the heap of tissue and bone that had once been a man. A man of faith. It resembled no man any longer. And for the first time, after seeing countless bodies in grim and morbid variations and decomposition, she knew she was going to be sick. She stumbled to the flap and emptied her morning coffee with wet heaves and then dry, dry painful heaves onto the ground.

She took deep breaths trying to calm her mind and stomach and then Drake's hand emerged from the flap with a wet cloth that he pressed into her own.

Back inside the tent, Drake had placed a cup of cool water on the front table for her. She drank all of it in loud gulps and he took the cup and turned to refill it. "I've seen this only once before," he said, "in mainland China, a small village of farmers and fisherman. I was a visitor, the guest of a man I had met earlier at a trade station. It was the cusp of spring, still bitter cold, but the world around us was thawing. Everywhere you could hear the trickle of water, like wind-chimes, the crackle of ice dissolving. I was passing through and the man welcomed me into his home with his wife and young son." Drake placed the filled cup in her hand. "His son was six, seven at the most. Kind-hearted people; they gave me shelter and I shared what food I had on me. I was only to stay overnight... my journey was at its end and my retrieval point was only twelve miles east of the village the following day."

Christina sipped at her water. It wasn't hard to imagine a wanderlust Drake sitting before a fire in a foreign land, with a family that seemed to instantly befriend him. The fire's flames would illuminate their smiles, perhaps with the child sitting in Drake's lap, looking up into his face with wide-eyed innocence. Wasn't hard to imagine at all the goodwill Drake would bring out in anyone. But she tried not to focus on the faces of the family, didn't want to put detail there when she knew there would be pain and dark shadows to follow—this story by Drake's own admission would end brutally.

"After the dinner hour, the man and I went out for more wood for the fire. It was a windy night, howling wind so that you had to yell to be heard two feet away. The pin where the family kept the wood was about twenty yards from the back of the house and where the rice fields began. That's where we found the chickens, only we wouldn't have recognized them if not for the creased feathers everywhere. The farmer thought he heard something in the fields and went after it, thinking it was what killed his chickens. I tried to call him back—he had no weapon to defend himself. I guess the man was just devastated over the loss; it's the difference between living and starving to death in some regions. So I followed best I could, but I didn't know the layout of the fields, not like he did, and we became separated fast with only that howling wind as company. You know, I'm a born tracker...my mother was Cherokee and my grandfather and uncles taught me to hunt with my senses. After a few minutes, I found my friend, his dark silhouette bent over something on the ground between two fallen trees. I called out to him and he turned—and just like that," Drake snapped his fingers, "he disappeared. Only it wasn't my friend standing there hovering over something, my friend was the one on the ground, a mangled mess. This dark figure...when it straightened, was too tall to be my friend, few men ever reach this height. Oh, I don't know, surely it was seven to eight feet tall, human shaped in the quick glance I got— but no man moves that fast. No way. It was like the Dark out-running the dark—a shadow outrunning its maker. And for all its attempts to blind me to it, to cloak itself in darkness and remain unseen, invisible, I had a fleeting moment of recognition. I don't even know how to explain it. A flash, deja-vu. I don't know...but I do know that what-ever it was, it was not of this world."

Christina sat still, the cup drained and table next to Drake's notebook. Without a doubt, Drake had told her much more than the notes he'd written, much more. She sighed. "I wouldn't tell *them* any of what you've told me." Christina knew Simon would just laugh in Drake's face and McClure was even likely to have Drake shot rather than take a chance on his sanity failing and endangering the unit after hearing a tale like the one she just had.

"That was never a possibility. They're hard-fact men. There's no place for the unknown in their shrunken little world." Drake assured her.

Christina smiled wanly. It was a compliment, that he'd shared the experience with her said as much. "I need to get back before they send someone for me." She rose from the chair, standing stiff and weary. Once she left Drake's tent the enormity of it all would threaten her sanity, she felt the burden was lifted in his presence. He made it bearable.

"Christina...I mean, Lt. Hannigan—"

"You may call me Christina. I don't mind."

"Most people call me 'Drake', but my first name is Michael."

Christina smiled. "I like Drake."

Drake nodded. "One more thing I think you should know." He paused, and ran his hand through his longish dark hair. "There was another visitor in the village that night. He came up missing that night also, around the time my friend was murdered...Christina, I believe that whatever did this is following me."

II

Sliding into Hell

The night wind howled through the stones as a lone figure sat among the tombs in Cobble's cemetery on its western shore. He wore all black and sunglasses covered his eyes from sight. The stars above reflected in their darkness. Days before he had set things into motion, in this very place with Deputy Gordon's blood. He looked around at the dug out graves and the long rotted bodies that littered the cemetery. Many months before a battle had been fought in this place, a battle for survival between the living and the dead. The men and women of this island had butchered his children sending most of them back to the eternal void in this very place. The few lucky enough to escape the islanders' perimeter had not been enough. This island had held, where the world had given way to his power. He doubted the people here knew they were the last of their species but it didn't matter. It would end here. He would see to that.

When the plague began all across the world, it had been the work of a virus. A virus he led humanity, in its arrogance and false wisdom, into creating for him. But this time, it had taken his power and work to bring about a second birth for his children here.

It was the only way and it had cost him dearly. He was weakened, weaker than he had been in thousands of years.

His strength would return in time however and his newly created "children" would grow stronger with each passing hour. They were his masterpiece and as he watched the corpses around him twitch and spasm, he knew it was worth it. Old wounds healed, brain tissue reformed, and the dead awoke once more. Their moans filled the silent spaces of the night and their voices so rich with pain and hunger cried out in the moonlight.

One of them staggered towards him. He reached out and caressed its grey flesh, knocking a swarm of feeding maggots from its face. "It's time," he whispered gently, "Go now and feed." He leaned forward and kissed the man-corpse's brow.

〜〜

Ellen Tucker stood on the front porch of her house staring out into the fields. Corn sprouted in long rows and soon it would be time for the harvest. It had been a good year for crops all across the island. Yet, it wasn't the coming winter and its worries that kept her outside in the cool night air. She pulled her jacket tighter about herself and shivered as breeze swept across the porch and fields. The sun had long since set and Ben had not returned. She was filled with a nervous energy and knew she wouldn't rest until Ben came home to her. She and Ben loved Cobble and were thankful that they made their home on the island but, she and Ben seldom went into town. They liked the peace, out here, far from even the small streets of the island proper. Their few trips were mostly to visit Martha and help out with the children she cared for or to deliver their produce to the island's stores since the plague had hit. Today, Ben had gone out because Terry had needed his help. She didn't know all the details but she knew that whatever had happened this morning was bad and terribly so. She sat down in a wooden rocking chair Ben had made the year before and turned her gaze to the vacant drive where Ben's truck normally sat. She prayed for their safety, not just Ben and Terry's but the whole island. She couldn't imagine the plague striking this place again but the military folks being out in Halsbrook field with their guns and experiments put her on edge. There was something that wasn't right about them being here now, showing up out of the blue as they had. Cobble had had its own share of bloodshed and she hoped it was over with and behind the island. "Lord, please let Ben come home," she whispered out loud giving her prayers breath.

∽≈

Private Dietz swung his heavy combat boots out of the jeep and stepped out onto the dirt road. His partner, Hudson, climbed out from the other side, picking up his M-16 from where it rested near his seat. They had stopped to stretch their legs. They had been out riding around the island most of the day and were on their way back to Halsbrook Field. The jeep's gas gauge showed the tank to be almost empty.

"This freakin' sucks," Dietz complained.

"Ah, come on, man, you know you dig drivin' around in circles," Hudson laughed, moving to the side of the road to relieve his bladder.

"It's not our job to look after these *locals*," Dietz lit up a smoke and leaned against the jeep. We shouldn't be out wastin' fuel like this. The captain's given enough of our stores away to these yokels already. Who f-ing cares if one of them got wadded up into a human pretzel anyway?"

"Coulda been one of us just as easily."

"Yeah, right," Dietz chuckled. "Base camp is the safest damn place on this island."

Hudson zipped his pants and walked over to Dietz. "The captain felt we needed to keep an eye out, take a look around. I can't say I blame him. We haven't found a place yet that was really safe, who's to say this island is any different?"

"How far do we have left to go to get back?"

"You're drivin' Dietz. What ya askin' me for?"

"You're the navigator man. Shit, get the map." Dietz ordered.

Hudson started to lean into the jeep and dig around in the junk that littered the seat for the map.

"What the frag is that?" Dietz asked.

"What?" Hudson asked, offering the map.

Dietz ignored him. "Listen."

A shuffling could be heard in the trees surrounding the dirt road. It seemed to come from all around them.

Dietz drew his sidearm, motioning for Hudson to get his rifle ready.

"Oh my God," Hudson whispered as the first of the creatures lumbered out of the tree line. There was no doubt it was dead. Its flesh was horribly wrinkled and tinted with a green hue. Strands of kelp hung from its body and the starlight above reflected off the milky white pupils of its eyes. Others followed it. Some dressed in once fine suits and dresses which they had been buried in now long rotted and tattered, some dressed in fresher clothing but bearing the wounds of some kind of battle. Bullet holes riddled some of their bodies while others seemed to be missing large chunks of flesh. One dressed in a red flannel shirt, its throat torn open with pieces of flesh and tendons dangling from the opening lunged at Dietz. Dietz blinked, barely raising his Beretta in time to put a round into its forehead. The thing dropped to the gravel of the road and lay still. The echoing shot seemed to drive those around it into a frenzy. Hudson opened up with his rifle not bothering to take aim. He didn't care if the things went down to stay, just that he pushed them back from where he stood. By now the road in front of the jeep was filled with the creatures. There was no way through them. Dietz carefully placed two more shots before hopping into the back of the jeep as the creatures on his side forced him to retreat. He looked down at Hudson, who was slamming a fresh clip into his rifle. "Holy shit, what the Hell are we going to do?"

"Get on the radio! We've got to warn the captain!"

Like a child, one of the things stepped up to Hudson and plucked his rifle from his hands while the soldier still struggled to ready it. Hudson stared wide eyed into the thing's face in horror. It leaned forward and embraced him dropping the rifle. He screamed as its teeth ripped through his uniform into his shoulder. He shoved it back but the thing held onto him dragging him with it to the road.

Dietz watched as Hudson vanished beneath a sea of moaning, hungry mouths.

Dietz slid down into the driver's seat, grabbing the radio. He knew he was dead. There were too many of the things. He was determined to reach the Sarge, Captain Simon, anyone and let them know that the dead were here on the island. He felt cold hands tugging at him, fingernails digging into his skin and clawing at his hair as he managed to get the radio turned on in time to scream one final time.

❧≈

As the duty officer reported to McClure, the sergeant stared at him in disbelief. Finally, McClure asked, "Are you sure?' When the soldier nodded, McClure bolted from the tent without looking back. He ran across the camp in a vain search for the Captain. He noticed Christina emerging from Drake's tent. She looked pale as if she had been through a lot but McClure didn't give a damn. She was a soldier and though she outranked him, Simon had left him not her in command in this field.

"Hannigan!!" He yelled, "The shit just hit the fan. Get your gear."

"What are you talking about McClure?" she snapped back.

"Something's happened to Dietz and Hudson."

"What? What happened?"

"How should I know?" McClure shook his head. "They just radioed in but they weren't giving the report of the island like Simon asked for. They were screaming...I would wager money they're dead, Hannigan."

"It's started here too..." she muttered.

"Look, whether it's those dead things or this new killer the Captain's in an uproar about, either way, we have got to get ready to deal with it. Get your shit together woman and get this camp on full alert." McClure glanced at Drake's tent and nodded towards it. "He in there?"

"Yes."

"He's the best damn pilot we've got. I want him in the

air now! Tell him to take one of the Apaches and find out what the Hell happened to Dietz and Hudson."

McClure stormed off yelling orders at every one in the camp as he passed them.

Christina opened the flap of Drake's tent and leaned back inside, "I guess you heard..." she started and then stopped, blinking. The tent was empty.

Dr. Paxton came running up to her. "I have to get to my lab in town," he pleaded. "You have to take me."

She pushed Drake from her mind. He could take care of himself. Paxton shoved a set of keys into her hand. They belonged to the company's only other jeep.

"I'm serious, Christina," Paxton urged. "McClure gave his approval. He knows how vital my work is to us all."

Her grip tightened on the M-16 in her hand until her knuckles turned white but she kept the rage inside her in check. She slung the rifle onto her shoulder by its strap and started walking to the edge of the field and the sole remaining jeep. Paxton rushed on ahead of her as soon as he saw that she had agreed to take him.

⁓⁓

Things were moving. McClure looked behind him at the bustle of activity in the camp and smiled. The people of this unit were professionals; there was no doubt about it. Everyone was awake and ready for action, they were ready for anything.

McClure stood at the edge of the camp, he turned towards Sheridan Road. He could just see the headlights of Christina and Paxton's jeep slashing the darkness of the night as it bounced down the gravel road towards Cobble proper. He needed to radio Simon and let him know what was going on but batteries were so rare that the unit only had two working handsets, one of them now lost with Dietz, and the other still in the camp. He debated sending a messenger into town after Simon. The wind howled in the night around him. Something about it sounded odd and familiar. Then it hit him. It wasn't the wind that howled and moaned through the trees around Halsbrook field.

He ran to the camp's perimeter and strained his eyes as peered at the tree line. As he saw them his breath caught in his chest. It simply couldn't be, but it was.

All around the camp, from every direction, they came. It looked like there were a couple of hundred of them, maybe a good deal more. The dead had come back to Cobble.

Other soldiers in the camp had seen them too and were readying their weapons. All of them looked to McClure for what to do. Would they try to hold their ground or pull out?

McClure motioned at one of the closest of his men who tossed him a rifle. "Let's show these damn F-ers how welcome they are here," he growled.

Thanks in part to McClure's own sense of paranoia and in part to Simon's "by the book" attitude of setting up camp, the unit was firmly dug in. Foxhole like firing positions lined the camp's edge and a few carefully placed claymores waited in the field between the tree line and the camp for the oncoming dead.

Explosions ripped the night as the waves of the dead poured through the small line of mines. McClure watched dozens of them fall, shredded by the shrapnel. The men and women of his unit had taken their positions around the camp to face the charge.

He raised his M-16 to his shoulder where he stood and took careful aim. His shot splattered the head of one of the leading creatures to pulp which rained onto the grass as its body toppled.

The dead charged onward toward the camp despite the losses they had taken to the mines, they didn't have enough reasoning left in their rotting heads to think there could be more mines or care. The unit's fire filled the field with even more bodies as well but the ranks of the dead were just too many and McClure realized the encampment was going to be overrun. There were already breaches in the perimeter on two sides.

McClure watched the things actually run towards the camp. These were *not* the dead he'd fought all across the mainland. These things moved like humans, fast and deadly.

The screams of those under his command were coming from all around him now. The dead were inside the unit's lines. McClure flipped his rifle to full auto and swept it over the ranks of the creatures coming towards him until it clicked empty. He tossed it aside and retreated into the camp, drawing his sidearm. He noticed Private Stacy wrestling in hand to hand combat with a creature to his right. He watched the young pilot swinging his empty weapon like a club at the corpse.

An explosion knocked McClure from his feet as one of the copters went up in flames. Some idiot was inside one of the Apaches and had opened up its main guns straight into the camp. Scores of the dead were killed by the copter's weapons but unfortunately the barrage had also struck the transport bird nearest to it and set off a chain reaction. Another bird blew as fire rained into the chaos of the battle.

McClure rolled to his feet cursing the damned fool who's just wiped out half of their fleet and came up staring at a man dressed in a tattered tux right in his white, unfocused eyes. The man's lower lip dangled from his face, barely attached, and a long string of puss dripped from his chin. McClure was so close to him that he reached out and pressed the barrel of his pistol to the thing's dead flesh before he pulled the trigger.

McClure staggered towards one of the last copters, a huge transport bird that was on the other side of the camp from the rain of fire. He struggled with its cargo door and forced it down climbing inside, locked it behind him. He raced to the pilot seat, plopping into it, and cupped his hands over his mouth and nose as he stared out into the sea of dead. Rotting hands pounded on the bulletproof glass of the bird's window from below its cockpit as he watched the tide of death sweep over him and past him towards the other end of camp.

The sounds of gunfire were sporadic now. None of the surviving copters had taken off either. He hoped some of his personnel might be lucky enough to survive and make it into to town. The bird he was in had been slated for repairs to its guidance systems and was not flight capable. McClure swore as he tried to ignore the pounding on the cargo door behind him and the way the copter rocked in its position from the mass of creatures outside it trying to find or tear a way inside to get at him. He could see the fingertips of groping hands at the bottom edge of the helicopter's forward window and the moans and howling around the vehicle seemed to be growing in intensity as the sounds of gunfire in the camp had grown almost silent now. McClure picked up the radio and tried to find the sheriff's frequency. However much he hated the islanders, however jealous of them he was for their paradise here, he hated the dead more. They had to be warned of what was on its way to town. The dead would not be stopping here.

⊷⊷

The thunderous gunfire had given way to silence outside the tent, and huddled inside the center of the tent with hands still clamped to their ears and eyes still desperately closed, the children waited for Paxton or someone to return. Quiet children in the eye of the hurricane waiting for instruction, and when none came from the adults outside the tent, Caleb stood on trembling legs.

The younger children looked up at him with bright eyes of unshed tears. Children of the Plague generation knew when to listen, when to act, and when to follow the older children. They were a generation inherent of survival and wit. Even the younger children were taught endurance and camouflage. What to do and not do in the face of an attack with the undead or living. Because in extreme times of crisis, lines got blurred, life and death as a matter of biological threat was subject to change. Isaac and Ingrid, especially, had learned that lesson from experience.

Now Caleb motioned to Marcus, who was a year younger than himself. They would search the tent for weapons and protect themselves and their smaller brothers and sisters from whatever threat lie outside, live or undead. They found two 9 millimeter handguns in holsters on the uppermost shelf in a rust-scarred medical supply cabinet. Sepia-colored bottles lined the rest of the cabinet's shelves and Caleb took one down and read the label. Without a word, he pointed for Marcus to read what he'd discovered, then both slid a bottle into their windbreaker pockets. A light touch on his arm, a gentle squeeze, and Caleb turned to see that Ingrid had found a bowie knife sheathed in leather beneath Paxton's personal affects in his desk. She held it up to him on outstretched palms as if an offering. He smiled and smoothed her ratted hair back from her face. One of the other kids, a round-faced boy named Trent, found a flare gun in a locker with Paxton's boots, hardly a formidable weapon, but it might come in handy he thought.

Three weapons. If the army with all their fire power couldn't stop whatever was rushing the camp, how pathetic were two guns and a knife? But he was not allowed the luxury of doubt for the silence was suddenly shattered by the real storm. They'd passed the eye into another realm of madness as the first of many torturous screams pierced and reverberated through the night air. Worse than crackling machine gun fire, worse than the earlier explosion of the helicopters nearby, was the screaming pleads for help. They seemed to come from everywhere at once, engulfing the tent, and leaving no doubt in their young minds who'd won the battle for the camp.

Caleb opened the tent flap and looked out into the camp. The night was lit by the flickering fires which burned from the remains of a nearby copter. The undead were everywhere, all around them, but most of the things were busy enjoying the spoils of their victory. He watched three of the things clustered around the thrashing form of one of McClure's men. The things were peeling strips of flesh from the man's dying body and shoving it into their greedy mouths. Caleb knew they had to make a break for it now while the creatures were still feeding or it would be too late. In that instant, he knew also what he had to do.

He grabbed Marcus and whispered into the younger boy's ear. Marcus pulled away staring at Caleb in horror. "No!" Marcus shouted. One of the creatures outside turned its head toward them looking them over with white clouded eyes and began to stumble towards the tent. "It has to be this way! Get going!" Caleb ordered and shoved Marcus out of his way.

Caleb ran straight towards the creature. He raised his pistol and fired wildly at it. Some of his first rounds went wide but two struck the thing in its chest and knocked it from his path. He tore by it, yelling an incoherent battle cry at the top of his lungs. All around the camp, the dead stopped and whirled to watch him. Caleb leapt over the body of a solider lying in the dirt with his stomach ripped open and darted out of the camp for the trees.

Marcus, gritting his teeth in anger, watched Caleb disappear into the night with the bulk of the creatures moving after him. Marcus turned and motioned to the other children. As one, they broke from the tent and ran in the opposite direction Caleb had run. Marcus prayed as he clenched his 9mm pistol white-knuckled in his hand that he could get the others to town so Caleb's life wouldn't have been given in vain.

≈

Christina stopped the jeep. She and Paxton sat looking back at the base in the hills above them. The sounds of gunfire which echoed in the night moments before were gone now and flames could be seen, burning inside the camp. They were too far away to clearly see what had happened but Christina could make a good guess. Paxton rubbed at his face with his hands, mumbling something about his lab in the passenger seat.

Christina's eyes were hard. She didn't know whether to turn back and try to help McClure or head on into town. In her moment of trying to decide, Paxton yanked the 9mm from her side holster and took the choice out of her hands. The doctor caught her so off guard she had no time to react as he lashed out with the butt of the pistol and spilt the skin of her scalp open with a heavy blow to the side of her head. Christina's limp body fell forward onto the wheel and the jeep's horn sang in the darkness. Paxton kicked her body from the vehicle and slid into the driver's seat.

He left her lying in the dirt without looking back as he gunned the gas, slinging gravel as the jeep shot towards town.

～～

Terry's car squealed into the parking lot outside the marina. The docks were packed with boats which rocked on the waves, gathering dust, unused. The lights in Robert's office were on and Terry watched him run out to meet them as he and Ben got out of the patrol car.

Terry didn't give him time to argue. He moved towards the pumps with a jug in his hands. To Terry's shock however, Robert didn't protest. Instead, Robert just stared at him. It was so disturbing Terry turned to face him and started to offer an explanation as to why he needed the fuel but Robert spoke first. "Terry, what are we going to do?"

Terry stood there speechless, eyeing Robert as Ben took the jug from Terry's hand and went onto to get fuel for the car.

"I...I was listening to the radio," Robert babbled. "And, I heard, I heard..."

"Robert," Terry asked carefully, "Are you alright, man? There hasn't been anything on the radio since we lost touch with the mainland."

"Not that radio, Sheriff. I was listening to the frequency that military group uses. They're dead. All of them."

"Robert, what are you talking about?"

"Their base up in Halsbrook field was just overrun. The dead have come back to Cobble, Sheriff, and they're on their way to town right now, hundreds of them. There was this guy. I think he kept saying his name was McClure, who kept calling for you over and over until there was this smashing sound, like glass shattering then all he did was scream and the frequency went to just being static."

Terry walked back over to the patrol car and fiddled with his radio, turning to the band used by Simon's unit. All he got was static. It wasn't that unusual. Simon's unit was small and under equipped but none-the-less, the silence added some credence to Robert's claims. Terry looked over at Ben who was returning with the gas. It was clear he had over heard what Robert had said. He met Terry's gaze and shrugged.

Terry picked up his radio. He had to check things out and Simon was supposedly still in town so he might be able to reach him, at least second hand, and find out what, if anything was indeed going on.

~∾~

After dropping off Ensley's corpse at Paxton's lab in town then staying to see the body sent out to the make-shift labs in Halsbrook field for Lieutenant Drake to continue studying it, Simon had spent his day in the company of Mayor Beck. Beck had given Simon a brief tour of the island and explained a lot of things about Cobble, how it had survived the plague, and its history. Simon endured it all with a smile. Now, the two men sat across a desk from each other in Beck's study. The old man's home was rather elaborate compared to others on the island and Simon was forced to admit Beck was more capable than he appeared. The man was a master at manipulation and shrewdly cunning. Had Beck been younger, Simon might have had him disposed of to be on the safe side. But as he was, losing his control over Cobble more and more with each passing day to Terry, Simon didn't consider him a threat to his plans to make Cobble his own. If anything, so far, Beck served as an unexpected ally.

Beck poured them each another glass of wine from the decanter which rested on top of the desk and Simon took the offered glass leaning back in his chair. Simon swirled the wine around in his glass, savoring its rich smell.

"So, you'll do it then?" Beck asked.

"Of course, that snot nosed sheriff of yours has been nothing but a pain in my ass since we got here. Hell, I would have done it even without your generous offer, Mayor."

Beck's wrinkled lips part in a smile. "Good. I am glad we could reach an agreement."

Simon started to take a sip from his wine and almost

choked on it as he caught a sign of movement outside the study's window. Something flashed by it in a blur. Beck noticed it too from the corner of his eye and the old man spun in his chair to try to get a look.

A crash sounded from the living room outside where the house's front door was. Beck jumped from his seat as he heard his wife screaming.

Simon sat his drink down and drew his sidearm. No panic showed in his stone features, only his determination to stay alive. He'd been through enough things like this in his career to harden him to the unexpected and he was prepared to deal with it whatever it may be.

Beck moved to head out into the house after his wife and Simon caught him by the arm. Simon looked into Beck's eyes and shook his head, motioning the old man to remain silent.

Beck jumped as a knock sounded on the study door. Simon raised his handgun and put three rounds through the thin wood of the door. Each shot booming like a series of thunderclaps in the small room. Then everything was still again. Slowly the door to the study slid open and Beck's wife toppled inside. Beck's face was a contorted mask of terror as he stared at her body. The flesh had been ripped from her face entirely and her mouth was locked open in scream. Her tongue dangled, barely still attached, hanging out over her teeth. Three bullet holes from Simon's shots leaked blood onto the front of her blue gown.

A man stood in the doorway. He smiled at them as if nothing about the scene were out of place and stepped over Beck's wife as he entered. "Good evening, gentlemen. I trust I am not interrupting?"

Beck howled with anger and leapt at the man who lashed out, backhanding him across the room. Beck's form hit the opposite wall of the study with a thud and the crunching sound of old bones breaking. His body slid down to rest unmoving in the floor. Blood leaked from his ears and nose and his eyes though open showed only white and were rolled up inside his skull.

Simon held his gun pointed carefully at the intruder.

"Look, I have no quarrel with you," Simon stated. "Just get out of my way and neither of us will have to die here tonight."

The man laughed. "Oh but I have a quarrel with you, Captain."

"I don't even know you." Simon answered through gritted teeth.

"No, but you're alive," the man's tongue shot out of his mouth like a snake wrapping around Simon's throat before the veteran soldier could move. Simon felt its roughness cutting and slashing his skin but he managed to keep his aim and pull the trigger. His round caught the man dead in the center of his forehead blowing brain matter out onto the hallway carpet outside the study. The man didn't even flinch though. He merely recoiled his tongue and laughed. Simon rubbed at his neck and fired again, emptying his clip, but the man was already gone by the time Simon's bullets reached where he had been standing. Simon felt someone embrace him from behind. "Goodnight my sweet captain," a voice purred into his ear before the cracking sound of every bone in Simon's body echoed through the study and the night fell quiet once more.

~⁊❦~

In the flickering light of the candles that lit her kitchen, Amy tried again. She'd been calling on the radio for her father for the last half hour. She knew something was terribly wrong on the island. She could feel it. She needed her father. She needed him here to make her feel safe and know things were going to be ok but she also needed him because she knew if she died like this, left alone, like her mother had, Terry wouldn't be able to live through it. "Dad, please answer me. Gordon, are you there? Please...somebody answer me," Amy pleaded with tears in her eyes.

"Hello, Amy," a husky masculine voice answered, unfamiliar to her.

"Yes. Who is this?" and then because really, what did it matter when the radio had been unreliable all evening—

"I'm trying to contact the sheriff. I'm his daughter. Can you tell me if—"

"I would love to discuss it with you, Amy. And all you have to do is come outside. Right outside the door."

Her hand squeezed the radio mouthpiece. Something about the voice caused her to shudder, made her cold inside. "Who is this? How do you know my name?" and uncertain now but she asked regardless, "Did my dad send you?" She peeked out the window, through the tiniest fold of the curtain she could see a shadowy figure leaning against the porch column.

"That's right. Now open the door. I'm here to protect you."

She eased to the heavy door, her hand finding the first of several strong bolt-locks. She'd made her mind up. *Listen to your instincts*, Terry had told her countless times. *When in doubt, gut instincts rarely fail you.* The windows were barred securely, another example of the times they lived in. Her hand shook as she slid the final bolt in place at the top of the door. The voice sighed.

"My father would never send someone I didn't know."

"Amy..."

"Please leave."

"Amy," the voice was more insistent. And muffled.

Beneath the door, the tip of something began to wedge through the narrow space. Oily-black and writhing, the tapered tip fed its length as if threading the loop of a needle, whipcord-lean and searching, feeling its way: two inches, then three, four...

The gun rack stood beside the sofa, all within loaded and ready. She grabbed a rifle and a smaller pistol, then quickly crossed to the kitchen to take the butcher knife from the block. Her heart raced, yet she handled her weapons with confidence. Last stand mentality with a clear head as she had been taught. She tried not to think of what the intruder's use of her father's radio meant, tried to concentrate on the here and now of her own predicament: the slither of the strange tentacle-like object underneath the door searching for her; the undead didn't acquire body parts they didn't have while still alive...What was she dealing with here?

The snaking appendage was now at least four feet inside the living room. It coiled and lashed out, then grew still except for a slight sway back and forth, seeming to taste the air. She took a careful step toward it, the knife raised in counter-position. The swaying motion turned into a hypnotic wave. Amy's eyes blurred as she watched it; numbness was creeping into her head making it harder to focus. Whispers filled her ears—nothing coherent—just breathy murmurs through static, lulling. Turning her arms, her legs, to rubber. The rifle fell from her hand, banging against the wooden floor. The arm that held the knife fell to her side, the smooth handle sliding from her loose grasp little by little even as she tried desperately to make a fist around it. She tottered on legs that no longer felt solid or capable of supporting her weight. Her vision was now darkening at the edges, crowding inward. The last thing she heard was the sound of shattering glass. It drowned the frantic whispers that had become one with the encroaching darkness.

⁊≋

Drake had waited in the cover of trees. He waited as his nemesis spoke through the radio, hearing the girl called Amy deny the monstrosity disguised as a man outside her door. Poised for action, he stood and watched as the serpent tongue unfurled from the demon's mouth, watched as the demon's head bent back, arms held out from his sides, legs spaced apart—a human pentagram. Except he wasn't human. Drake had known that for years now.

When the demon's tongue had breached the door, he decided to make his move. He side-stepped from the trees, crouching low to the ground and walked the fifty yards to position himself to the rear. He then aimed the nine millimeter squarely in the back of the demon's head and squeezed the trigger.

The demon's body jolted; the tongue withdrew from underneath the door instantly. And then all the windows in the house had exploded like additional gunfire.

≈≈

Amy was aware that she was being carried. Through the haze of regaining consciousness: the jarring sensation of moving fast, the labor of heavy breathing, and the sound whuff-whuff-whuff of a pounding heartbeat. She blinked in surprise, confused to see the dark canopy of trees overhead, startled at the slap of branches scraping and stinging her arms and legs, getting caught in her hair. She strained to remember what had happened: the man; the disgusting tentacle; the shattering glass...there was the rifle and the knife, but now her hands were empty except for clutching at the man who held her as he ran. It wasn't the intruder, of this she was sure, and her arms tightened around his neck in relief. She couldn't see his features in the obliteration, but oddly felt she could trust this man. He'd saved her, after all. But it was more than that. More than what the facts portrayed. Just as her instincts had warned of the nature of the intruder, they now soothed her in the presence of her rescuer. Undoubtedly she was safer with him. Maybe her dad had sent this man for her. Maybe he was still alive. Hope filled her as she spoke. "I can run. You don't have to carry me anymore."

≈≈

Terry had been unable to contact Simon on the radio. In fact, Terry hadn't been able to reach anyone on any frequency he had tried. Almost instinctively, Terry realized somewhere inside himself that the day he had always hoped to never see again had come.

The dead were back on Cobble or perhaps even something worse. He was torn. His heart screamed out at him to go see to Amy. He had lost her mother defending the island in the early days of the plague by not being there for her but had he not made that sacrifice then all of Cobble including Amy would surely have been lost. Now, it came down to the line again and he was forced to decide between being Sheriff and being a father. So many people were counting on him to keep them alive.

Ben and Robert stood watching him sitting in the

driver's seat of his patrol car, the radio dangling in his hand, with a tortured look like that of man in Hell locked on his face.

"Terry?" Ben asked. When Terry didn't respond, Ben neared him and placed a hand on his shoulder. "Terry, you need to go home. I can handle things here with Robert's help. We'll get the supplies we need and get everyone into the town hall. I think it would be the best place to make our stand."

Terry looked up at him, his eyes still showing that he didn't fully register Ben's words.

"Terry, take the car and go see to your daughter," Ben ordered.

Terry nodded, sliding the rest of the way into the vehicle. He closed the door and looked back at Ben with both gratefulness and an understanding of what Ben was risking himself. Ellen would be alone now at their farm. As Terry drove off, he prayed for Ben and Ellen as he drew his .38 from his holster and flipped it open to make sure it was ready. Hell had returned to Cobble.

❧

Ellen Tucker had long given up on Ben's return. She was in the process of getting ready to make the walk into town when she heard the dogs start barking. She dropped the backpack of things she had been assembling for her hike and snatched up one of Ben's hunting rifles. Ellen stepped back out on the porch. The dogs were chained up to the left of the house and they appeared to have gone mad. They tugged at the leashes which held them and barked violently at the fields in front of the house.

Ellen strained her eyes in the darkness trying to see what they were so upset about. As she did so, the first of the creatures came bursting of the rows of corn and ran directly at her. It was a man who looked to have been in his mid-forties when he died wearing what appeared to be a tattered business suit. His face was contorted in a snarl of rage and his skin was covered in black patches of rot and dirt. Ellen swung the rifle's butt upwards at the man as he leapt up the small set of steps leading up to the porch. It caught him under the chin and knocked him backwards. Four more things like him had already emerged from the fields, coming towards her, and she could see the tops of the corn moving all the way across the field into the distance. Ellen darted back into the house and slammed the door behind her. She locked it and leaned her back against its frame. Terror ripped through her. The worst was becoming a reality. The rifle clattered to the floor. She slid to the floor and covered her mouth with her right hand. She wondered if Ben was dead and that was why he hadn't returned. There were dozens of those things out there. Were they all over the island again?

She realized suddenly that there was no way she could lock all the doors and windows before the creatures reached them and even if she could they wouldn't hold the things out, there were far too many of them.

Ellen jumped as something slammed hard into the door behind her. She heard a sound like a half moan, half scream come from the other side of the door, then the pounding started. The door shook from the blows of the thing outside.

Ellen reached over and picked up the rifle again. She held it with white knuckled hands. The back door to the house crashed inward and from where she sat she watched the things pouring into the kitchen.

Ellen crossed herself and placed the rifle in her mouth like Ben had taught her. She closed her eyes and squeezed the trigger softly. The rifle kicked as blood sprayed onto the door frame.

~~

Warning sirens blared throughout the streets of Cobble as Terry drove towards his home. The sirens were loud, jury-rigged, and ancient. They were a precaution Terry had put in place months before with the help of other men in the town. Right now, Cobble sounded like London during the bombing raids of World War II. No one in the town could sleep through their blaring. Terry was happy to know that Ben had been able to get them started. At least everyone in town would have some warning before whatever was about to happen went down. He just hoped Ben could round up everyone and get them to the town hall quickly enough.

Terry pulled into his driveway and bolted from his car, running towards the house. His heart stopped in his chest as he got close enough to see the front door. The door lay crooked on its hinges and the wood was splintered inward as if someone had driven a large stake through it. His eyes moved to the shards of glass that covered the lawn and the black, slime ooze that was smeared over his front steps.

"Amy!" he screamed into the night. As if in answer, he heard something off to his right in the woods. He forgot about the house, not daring to enter it, and dashed into the trees after the noise.

⌇◞❧

Ben Tucker stood outside the town hall. The street in front of it was packed with people. Men, women, and children poured into the building in a chaotic stream, fighting with each other to get inside first as if just being inside its walls was going to save them.

Ben knew everyone here had a lot of work to do and almost no time to do it in.

The town hall had been stocked and readied to a degree for something like this during the first weeks of the plague long ago. Its basement was filled with supplies ranging from fuel for its generators to preserved food to ammunition. It was the fortifications and the people where all the work lay. Ben had to get everyone calmed down and working together or they would never be ready in time if the dead were back and coming for them. The doors had to be boarded up and reinforced once everyone was inside and he hoped to have gunmen up on the roof in place to hopefully stop the dead from reaching the door at all if the creatures' numbers were small enough. Ben didn't have a clue how the dead had came back, but he imagined there couldn't be that many of them. He had been part of the group of men with Terry at the cemetery when the dead had first awakened on Cobble. He knew Cobble's dead had been dealt with because he had done part of it himself. On the bad days, he could remember the inhuman screams, the echoes of the gunfire and running chainsaws that had filled the graveyard. He could even still smell the smoke and stink of blood on him from that day at times. Ben shook his head and yelled at Robert who was trying to break up a fight between two men over an automatic weapon from the hall's stash they had passed out earlier. This was going to be one Hell of a job. Ben just hoped he could handle it and hold things together until Terry got back with Amy.

❧

When Paxton reached his lab, he knew instantly something was wrong. The flickering light of candles could be seen inside the house the islanders had lent him to work in. The young doctor hopped out of his jeep and marched up to the front door with the pistol he'd taken from Christina at the ready.

The light seemed to be coming from his lab itself and not his office so that's where he headed. The old man named Jared awaited him, sitting in the middle of the lab in a wooden chair facing the doorway. As Paxton entered, Jared watched him carefully. The old man held a pistol of his own in his withered hands.

"Paxton," Jared said with disgust clear in his voice.

"Doctor," Paxton answered back in a mocking tone that made it clear he thought the old man's title was a joke. Paxton's eyes scanned the contents of the room. He noticed his file cabinet had been forced open and his papers lay scattered across the floor.

When he looked back to Jared, the old man met his stare with one just as icy.

"I think it's time we had that talk I promised a while back about the children, Mr. Paxton," Jared raised his gun and leveled it at Paxton's chest. "I want to know why you're here, all of you and I want to know what you were planning to do to our children."

Paxton laughed. "Tell me Jared in all this time are you any closer to understanding the plague and how it works?"

Jared didn't answer. He merely kept his gun trained on the younger man.

"You want to know why I came to this place. Well, first you must understand some things about the plague." Paxton began to explain his theory of the plague virus.

"The virus causes the dead cells of a body to become re-animated. It seems these infected cells take directives from a different host—not just a high-jacked cell, but an independent organism." Paxton continued, "Let me clarify in case this is too advanced for you: Instead of each individual cell passing instructions to the next, corrupting the cell—as any virus does—it passes a mechanism for some sort of outside command to take over. Essentially, these walking dead, or re-animators—as those in the military call them—are taking orders. From whom, I've no idea. But there is an outside source and I believe it to be on this island as we speak. I believe this person or creature or whatever it is was responsible for the death of your island's priest. Of course we had no way of knowing the "controller" of the plague was here when we set out for Cobble. No, I personally wanted Simon to bring us here because I knew there would be children untouched by the plague here. I've learned that children are very resistant to the virus up until a certain age. I had been working with blood samples from the children to find a link; it had been suggested that perhaps a certain T-cell is responsible. My problem before coming to Cobble was that most of the mainland children were killed in the war or by the re-animators, or have gone underground. The children here were to be the perfect subjects to allow me to continue my work so I could find a way to interrupt these instructions that pass to the cells of the dead and as thus bring the virus or plague if you will to a halt entirely. Right now we know of no known antibiotic that will even phase the virus. Finding a way to halt the communications between the originator of the virus and the infected is our only hope of returning the world to normal."

"And your Captain had no objections to these experiments on children?" Jared asked in disbelief.

"Simon?" Paxton laughed again. "Ha, all Simon wanted was to escape the hell of the mainland and perhaps find a nice, comfortable place to set himself up as king of what was left of our race. Cobble was perfect for him as well. He figured you hicks would be easily manipulated and if not, well, he was prepared for that too. Now are we going to continue arguing or are you going to help me get the data I have collected out of here and to a safe place? In case you haven't noticed, it seems Hell has sprung up around us even here on your precious island."

Jared's gun hand trembled as he fought to control his rage. Paxton saw his answer in the old man's stance so he made the first move. He jerked his own pistol up. Shots rang inside the lab, a series of popping noises. When things fell quiet again, Paxton stood over Jared's body on the floor as blood pooled around it. The old man was dead. Paxton took a few steps towards his files scattered all over the floor trying to collect them. As he reached for them his chest tightened with pain. Only then did he take notice of the growing red stains on the front of his own white shirt. He toppled down on top of the files. As he lay there, he opened his mouth to say something, and blood leaked out. He swallowed hard. Someone had to save his work, he thought, it was mankind's only hope. He rolled onto his back as the rise and fall of his chest slowed and stared at the ceiling as the darkness of death flowed over him and took him in its arms.

❦

Half an hour later, Terry still hadn't shown up. Ben walked through the rows of islanders packed inside the hall trying to ignore the desperate eyes that followed him. Everyone seemed to accept him being in charge as if he were the sheriff himself. Ben had given up hope of Terry ever returning. As far as he was concerned the only living people on Cobble were the ones inside this building. He had to face the fact he would never see Ellen again. It broke his heart but he had a new responsibility to those gathered here now and he knew what Ellen would have wanted him to do. Ben made his way to the hall's front entrance where Robert and several other men worked reinforcing the heavy wooden doors to make sure things were going as planned.

When Robert saw Ben approaching, he sat down his hammer and the small tin of nails in his hands and moved to meet him. "Ben, Beck's not here either."

"I noticed," Ben answered.

"Looks like by default you're in charge now. I just wanted you to know, I'll stand by you whatever happens here."

"Have you seen any of that military unit from Halsbrook field?"

Robert nodded. "One of them came in with our folk. He's hurt. Not a bite from one of those dead things," Robert added quickly, "at least he claims he wasn't bit and there were no signs that he was but he's pretty banged up. He could barely walk on his own. We moved him to the back with the women."

"So I take it we can't count on any help from them folks?"

Robert shook his head. "According to him, they're all dead up there, Ben. He talks like an army of those things just came out of the night and massacred all of 'em."

Robert stared at Ben.

"I know what you're thinking Robert, if there were enough of those things to take out a group of professional killers what chance in Hell do we have holding out here?"

Robert managed a laugh. "You could say that."

"We have to *try*. We may be all of us that are left. Anywhere."

"Holy Shit!" Tim screamed. He was staring out the only window on the ground floor of the hall. Robert and Ben raced to his side and peered out over his shoulder.

"Would you look at that?" Tim said in a state of near disbelief.

Terry's deputy, Gordon, stood in the street in front of the hall. His uniform was covered in dried blood and he limped awkwardly as he moved closer to the building. It was clear he was dead but when Ben caught his eyes, he saw something in them that scared the crap out of him.

Gordon's eyes burned with an intelligence Ben had never seen in any of the walking dead before. Gordon's gaze told him the deputy would be a force to be reckoned with.

Ben started to smash out the window with the butt of his rifle and drop Gordon right then and there but Robert caught his gun as he lifted it.

"We've got to get this place sealed up fast, Ben."

A smile seemed to spread over Gordon's face as Ben continued to stare at the dead man. Gordon raised his arms towards the stars and screamed, a hissing sound like air howling from a punctured tire. Behind Gordon, the street was suddenly filled with hundreds of the dead. They came running from all directions, from every street and alleyway. They were everywhere.

Robert jerked Ben out of the way as Tim slammed a thick table top up over the window. Other men leaped to nail it in place.

"The roof!" Ben ordered. "We've got to take some of them down or the fortifications will never hold!"

A couple of armed men dropped what they were doing and followed Ben and Robert as they raced up the stairs that led to the second floor and the roof beyond.

≈≈

Christina Hannigan stumbled through the forest. Her head was pounding from the knock she took from McClure, but she knew she had to push on and make her way back to the camp. The children were in Paxton's tent when she'd left and she had to make sure they were alright. Surely someone had saved the children. Remembering Paxton's dispassionate stance, and McClure's selfishness, she doubted either had given them a second thought. Her balance was affected. She ping-ponged between trees as her vision swam. The darkness had a floating feel to it. A good chance of a concussion, she thought. She stopped for a moment, leaned against a tree. If only she hadn't agreed to take McClure in the first place. And then ahead in the darkness, movement. Instantly she ducked behind the tree, her hands gripping the rough bark for support. Flashes of white. Whispers. She wondered if the concussion was bad enough that she was having hallucinations. But then Marcus turned around as if he sensed her presence, coming toward her in relief and stopping abruptly. His hand went to the side of her head, just over her ear. "You're bleeding," he said with surprise, after all the carnage he must have witnessed this night.

Looking behind him at the other curious faces peering around his shoulder, she said, "McClure. I think...I think I have a concussion." It was then that she realized who she was looking for in the group of kids. "Where's Caleb?"

Marcus explained the sacrifice Caleb had made for them by drawing the zombies away while they escaped. "We don't know if he made it or not." He shuddered. "The zombies were everywhere. His chances weren't too good."

Christina pursed her lips. Her eyes closed briefly to hide the sorrow. "Where are you heading?"

Marcus ripped the cotton of his tee shirt, a long ragged strip, and then gently but tightly tied it around the wound at her temple. "That will keep the gash closed and keep the bleeding to a minimal." He sighed and looked at the others. Lt. Hannigan and Private Drake were the only two people from the military invaders that the children had liked. She seemed kind and the honest sort, but he had all their lives to consider. He had a responsibility to their safekeeping and she was still an outsider. Besides, he really didn't know where they were going. His plan was just to get out of harm's way.

Christina understood his hesitation. "I only want to help," she whispered. "If you know of a safe place—let me go with you. I can't stay here in the forest."

"They're everywhere..." Marcus said, looking around as if expecting to see them hanging upside down from the tree branches. "And they're not like before...they're meaner, if that's possible. And faster. They can run like me and you."

❧❧

Caleb darted between the trees, running to gain distance from the leagues of undead that rushed on. He was a fast runner, his long legs gliding over the forest floor. The torn flesh of his shoulder hurt like hell when jostled but didn't hamper his pace. He'd been pursued while running from the camp, and then surrounded. The walking corpse of a woman had sprung from the vines and taken him down from behind, then buried her teeth in his shoulder. The burning pain of those teeth as they ripped through his skin and muscle was severe. He imagined it akin to how a shark attack would feel, the shaking and tearing of the victim's flesh. He didn't know if the burning was caused by the zombie itself or if he'd just never experienced a deep bite before...maybe there was something special about zombie spit, maybe it was like acid and burned all the way down to your bones...and blood. It hurt to think about it. Soon the infection would settle in and the mangled flesh would turn black and then the black rot would spread, fan out from the wound until all his skin was grey—then fever would begin and then rage until he could no longer keep a coherent thought in his head. He'd seen it all before. It really did him no good thinking about his fate, but he couldn't turn the thoughts off. He knew they would put him out of his misery when the fever had taken all rational thought—it seemed more humane that way, like they were waiting for the last shred of humanity to disappear before killing the beast. He also knew there was nothing to be done for it; the only thing keeping him going was the thought of the other kids' safety, of seeing Marta one more time and saying his good-byes, and using the last twenty-four hours of his life fighting the evil that had surfaced on the island. He had to concentrate on that, not his own fate. He couldn't believe the staggering numbers of undead. They were walking out of the ocean, nothing but skeletal remains in waterlogged rags; they were erupting from the ground, from beneath the wooden flooring of houses. He'd even watched as a corpse emerged from the tangled roots of a huge oak tree; it disentangled itself by wrenching free the vein-like roots with a strength no human could possibly have. He was so tired, if only he could stop and rest. But he needed to catch up with the group, there was a place he'd thought of that maybe the zombies couldn't follow. A horrible place. But what was more horrible than the disgusting creatures that pursued them—and the terrible things they would do once they caught him? No, there was no choice really. He couldn't circle back to town; that would mean a confrontation he couldn't win or outrun. There were no other options.

～

Terry slashed through the woods calling for Amy as he swung his flashlight back and forth. He spotted bits of cloth torn on low-hanging branches and shrubs, bits of her yellow blouse and strands of her auburn hair. He followed the trail but stopped calling out for her—if the enemy had taken Amy he didn't want to alert them of his presence. He now moved swiftly but quietly through the brush, trying to avoid the snapping of twigs. Once he got Amy back they would hurry back to the town with the others. He was needed there. But his first obligation was to his daughter and her safety. The town was the last stand.

The trail took him east toward the rocky beach, a remote area of the island. The foliage grew dense with vines and underbrush, the trail narrowing until Terry had to swipe his way between the trees and creeper. He had begun to worry that he'd lost the main trail, or maybe the abductor had changed directions, when he found Amy's shoe in a patch of hawthorn. He gripped the sneaker and picked up his pace.

The forest ended abruptly and the sand took over the ground. In the flashlight's circle of light he saw two pairs of footprints indenting the beach: a pair of large boots, and a pair of mismatched foot and sneaker prints. He followed their direction to the dark craggy cliffs overlooking the sea. He craned his neck to peer upward at the jutting ridges, thankful for the full moon that illuminated the peaks enough to distinguish that there was no silhouettes visible. The thought of Amy trying to climb the vertical cliffs made him queasier than he already was. Even if her abductor—and he no longer considered it kidnapping when it was apparent that Amy was following of her own freewill—was an accomplished climber, it could all go ter-

ribly wrong. One slip... But no, no he told himself. Amy
knew her limitations. Hadn't he taught her well? Besides,
he didn't think they would have had time to climb the
cliffs. Terry walked around the base of the formations. In
the past, this spot had been a place of refuge for the
undead. Now days people avoided the cliffs as it could
only rouse bad memories of finding loved ones here, of
having to deal with those family members or friends with
mercy and fire; in the bay of caves the charcoaled walls
still held ghosts if only in people's minds. He had to admit, though, it made perfect sense to use the area as a
hideout. He seriously doubted any of the undead were
around, but controlled the urge to shout her name anyway.

He climbed over a large boulder, then stopped to listen for any hint to where his daughter was hiding. Over
the uneven rocks, he fumbled, using his hands to feel his
way instead of the flashlight in an attempt to save the precious batteries. The moonlight was now on the other side
of the cliffs. Darkness was so prevailing that he couldn't
make a step without testing the ground first. He turned a
dark corner and something wafted across his face. He
heard the sound of breathing in the opaque blackness.
Hoping, praying, he called out "Amy?" and was nearly
knocked to the ground with the force of a body colliding
with his. "Dad!" And he hugged his daughter to him.

"I thought you were dead. Oh God, I thought you were
dead..."

Terry pulled back from Amy but still held on to her
thin shoulders. "Amy, who's with you?"

"Michael Drake. He saved my life."

A deep but mild voice spoke from behind her. "Sheriff," and Terry found his arm clutched in the dark, as Drake
shook his hand. "I'm on your side." Terry responded by
pumping the younger man's hand. "I can't tell you how
relieved I am to hear that. Thank you for saving my daughter. I owe you more than I can ever repay."

"I wouldn't have made it out without Drake. The Dark
Man..." and she told Terry what had transpired at their
home. Terry shuddered and hugged his daughter to him

once again. He'd come so close to loosing her. And although all might be lost on this night, he couldn't go on knowing he'd allowed something to happen to her. He would have lost all fight inside him and would be as good as dead.

Terry hugged Amy to him after hearing of her narrow escape. After a moment, he turned his attention to Drake. "Why do I have a feeling you know what we're dealing with here? Or at least more than we know, which is nothing really: a creature that embodies evil and," he thought about what Amy had said about the man's tongue, "has strange mutative abilities."

Drake let the silence stretch on. What he had learned about the creature that

Amy had begun calling "the Dark Man" was part intuition, like a dream handed down from a dream or collective memory from ancestor to ancestor, and part experience from glimpses from his past and the now of today. People had a hard time grasping dead people rising from the grave. How would they react to a being that was as mythical as Beelzebub himself? How would they comprehend a monster so vile, so seething with hatred that its ultimate goal was destruction of the soul of man? He didn't even understand it fully. It was like the first unsuspecting tingle along your spine, the hair-raising charge of electricity where every atom, every micron in your body knows of the lightning bolt a split second before it strikes. And as if an omen, the rumble of thunder sounded on the horizon.

The wind began to gust as Drake stood. "Come on, let's get inside the cave. I'll tell you what I know and don't know about the Dark Man."

≈≈

Caleb stopped when he heard something behind him; it was still in the not-so-far distance, cushioned from him, but coming up fast: *whoosh-whoosh* like a wind tunnel. With the crash of thunder overhead, he startled. Then suddenly the wind started to bluster and sway the boughs in the trees. A storm was coming. A fierce one. But the storm was a different entity; it wasn't what he heard pursuing him. It wasn't nature. It didn't sound natural—or healthy. His instincts told him to push on, and he stretched his gait and burst full speed ahead through low-hanging branches and snaking vines. He was looking over his shoulder, hearing only his huffing breath when he plowed into Marcus as he supported Lt. Hannigan. The three went sprawling to the ground. He helped the two up, gesturing wildly to the other children. "Let's go! Let's go! They're coming up behind me."

∿∿

Inside the dark cave, Drake used Terry's flashlight to find a thick dead tree branch. He ripped the inner lining of his fatigue jacket and wound it about the end of the branch creating a torch. From his pocket he fished matches and he lit it. "Won't last long," he said, "but we don't want to send smoke-signals, anyway."

Terry and Amy sat with their backs to the cave wall. With the torch's flame Terry could finally see his daughter's rescuer and recognized him instantly as the pilot that had accompanied lt. Hannigan the first day the military had showed up on the island.

Drake rested on one knee. "I don't have a name to put to him. Most would call him 'Devil' or 'demon'."

"Like the Christian Devil, the angel that was cast out of heaven?" Terry asked.

And Drake smiled wryly. "He's pretty much everyone's devil. From Buddhist to Atheist." Drake lowered his hand to the cave floor, took his index finger and drew a circle with a disproportioned triangle through its center, and in the corner of the triangle where it pierced the circle, he drew three strange symbols like hieroglyphics. "Do you recognize this symbol?"

Both Terry and Amy shook their heads.

Drake continued. "This is symbol is found throughout the world, in ancient artifacts and tomes." He pointed to the squiggles. "It means 'Eternal Death' and we don't know how far it dates back; it's baffling. But, the thing that is odd and mystifying is that the symbol for death is turned around backwards. Some scientists think that because it is backwards, it means the opposite. But what if, in light of this virus, we interpret the symbol as meaning both 'eternal death with eternal life'. That would explain this Armageddon we're seeing."

Amy craned her head. "But how do you know this is connected to the Dark Man?"

Drake lowered the torch to illuminate the symbol. "Because wherever I've found this symbol—in Damascus, Hanyang, Jerusalem, Istanbul, and various other places— I've encountered the Dark Man." He sighed. "I just know...and I don't know how to explain how I know. I feel taunted by him...It's more than a feeling, more like a conviction deep in my bones. And the dreams...they're not even really *my* dreams. I'm convinced that others have confronted this dark deity and I see it all played out through them, like collective memory." He gripped his scalp and tugged his hair slightly. "I don't expect you to believe what I'm telling you. It's hard enough to try and explain. All I know is it's out to wipe out mankind. This world plague comes at a time when this devil chooses to make himself known, seen. You have to see the correlation here. We are the only ones, *this* tiny little island, standing in his way..."

Terry threw out his arms halting the conversation. "Shhhh. Listen. Someone's coming."

Drake stamped the torch out and listened. He whispered to Terry and Amy to stay put and eased to the mouth of the cave. As the fog drifted along the ground, he made out several shapes in the faint moonlight. With a sigh of relief, he recognized the island's children and two of the older children were supporting Christina around their shoulders as they ran. He turned his head back to the cave to Amy and Terry, "It's the children. And Lt. Hannigan is with them" and stepped out of the cave to intercept them.

∽≈

Amy swept the hair back from Christina's face to look at the wound. "I'm not a doctor, but from the double vision and the lump you took, it appears to be a concussion. You probably shouldn't move around a lot."

Christina patted Amy's hand. "What a night to get a concussion, huh?"

"You're fortunate to have made it out alive, so consider it a lucky concussion," Terry said from the corner of the cave where he'd just spoken to Caleb. And then he took Amy by the arm. "I have to go back into town."

"Town? Well, I'm going with you. We're not separating now." Amy gestured at the cave. "We're in a half-way safe place. Why leave now? It doesn't make any sense." But she knew he felt guilty leaving the town to fend for itself. He took his job seriously, too seriously.

"That's why I want you to stay here. With Drake and the kids."

She was shaking her head. "I'm going with you."

Terry glanced over at Drake, his eyes pleaded for help with his headstrong daughter.

Drake set little Isaac down next to his sister, Ingrid, then took Amy's chin in his fingers. "I can't keep this all together without you. Christina's in no shape to help me mobilize the children if need be. And to be honest, there's no guarantee that we're safe here or for how long. They'll be looking for us, that much is guaranteed."

Amy's skin tingled under Drake's touch. He was the most mesmerizing man she'd ever met. She didn't want to leave him, but she couldn't let her father go alone either. Her emotions and loyalty were so torn...

Terry looked at the two of them. He hadn't realized it before, but there was something definitely there—and he was glad. He knew without a doubt that Drake would keep his daughter safe. He'd risked his life to save her before.

"Amy, please stay with Drake. I can't take you with me, not in good conscience. Make your old dad happy and stay where you're safe," Terry whispered.

"But you could stay here with us. You could—" her voice cracked.

Terry shook his head. "It's my town, sweetheart. I have to go."

"...I can't lose you..."

Terry hugged Amy to him. "I'll be back, just wait and see. We're going to rid ourselves of this curse and be bet-

ter than ever." He smoothed Amy's hair. "I'll see you soon."
He pulled away and kissed her on the forehead. "I love
you, Amy. Everything's going to be okay." And then he was
clasping Drake's hand before striding toward the cave's
entrance and out into the night.

"I love you, too," Amy called out after him.

≈≈

Terry left the cave without looking back. He was glad
Amy had found someone. A smile crept over his lips despite the darkness that seemed to lie ahead. Drake was a
good man. The military man had already saved his
daughter's life once. Somehow he knew it deep down that
there was nowhere on the island Amy would be safer than
in his company. Still a twinge of loss shot through him.
He doubted very much he would ever see Amy again and
hoped she knew just how much he loved her.

Terry made his way through the woods back to where
he had left his patrol car. When he reached it, there was
no sign of the dead around so he popped the trunk and
strapped a belt containing two fully loaded .38 revolvers
around his waist. He picked up a twelve gauge from the
confines of the trunk as well and pumped a round into its
chamber and double checked the weapon. Only then did
he move to get into the car, placing the shotgun within
easy reach in the passenger seat next to him. He cranked
up the engine and headed towards the center of town. He
knew Ben would have gathered everyone left alive into the
town hall by now. He just hoped they were holding out ok.

Terry didn't make it all the way to the hall before he
started encountering the dead. The small packs he passed
seemed to ignore him and were headed in the same direction that he was. The hall was most likely under siege by
now. He veered off the main road and pulled into the parking area of Robert's full depot once more. It was deserted
though a few unmoving bodies of the dead lay scattered
about.

He made sure the car's tank was full and picked up a
few items he thought he may need including a roll of duct
tape from Robert's office. He drove onward to a small hill

that overlooked the center of town. It was worse than he feared. The hall was surrounded by hundreds of the creatures and they seemed to be massed at the front entrance of the hall trying to force their way inside. The wind carried the sounds of gunshots from the hall's defenders to him and that at least was a good sign.

He looked around the pseudo-junkyard he stood in, which also had belonged to Robert before the plague though it now belonged to the island as whole as the concept of large scale personal property was an idea that had vanished with the bulk of the human race. The junkyard was primarily occupied by vehicles the islanders no longer had the resources to use. As one large truck caught his eye, a plan on how to get to the hall was born in his mind. He smiled, snatching up a can of gas and the roll of duct tape from his supplies. He wouldn't need much fuel for the truck. Laughing at the madness of his plan, he bounced a grenade in his left hand and set to work.

⋙⋘

Through the vast passages of time and civilizations, they had called him "Cryten", though the name was, for the most part, lost now in the new modern and aseptic world of organized religion. But by no means did that mean he was diminished in any way; he was lord over disease and pestilence and famine, greed and murder, all the black arts. He was the vessel in which all darkness sifted through, to be reborn and reborn again, eternal.

As he walked his eyes were accustomed to all variances of light or lack thereof—the opaque darkness and the dense trees of the forest should have hampered his progress, but he wasn't their mortal-kind and didn't have those limitations. In the weeks leading up to this night, he had developed beyond even his expectations: he could now sense each of his reanimated children—precisely where they were on the island—as well as the human animals yet to be contaminated (Oh, how he loathed them!—Even as he felt their energy strum and vibrate like electric discharges, saw in his mind's eye their pinpoint beacon) although that had been a slower process. And then there was the one creature he was destined to destroy: the humans' warrior, his final adversary, his nemesis throughout time and space and astral planes where matter and energy were but glowing essences in an evolving vortex of possibilities. After innumerous battles he was homing in on his prize. And in all the confrontations through the millennia between he and his foe, this was the first time he had his enemy's back to the wall, so close he could taste his victory. Fate had destroyed Drake's predecessor and father, before he could pass on important knowledge of the Eternal Battle. Not only was Drake ignorant of his heritage, he had no concept of the *true* power inherent inside him. Just the same, he had bided his time, treading carefully, after all Drake was still a dangerous foe simply by who he was. And now he quivered with anticipation. Drake was just up ahead, thinking to shield those insipid weak creatures in the cliffs and caves. It was time to show Drake just how weak and ineffectual he really was.

꿈

Ben, Robert, and a few other men bounded through the door leading to the hall's roof. Ben reached the roof's edge first and dropped into a firing position with his rifle braced against his shoulder. The others followed suit with Robert taking a spot next to Ben.

The streets below were filled with the dead and their ranks stretched out into the town of Cobble beyond where the gunmen even from their elevated position could see. The first of the dead had already reached the hall's entrance below and were slamming their rotting bodies against the hall's barred door. Waves of more dead poured towards the scene after them. Ben wasted precious seconds scanning the ranks of the dead for Gordon. He couldn't spot the deputy in the crowd below. Around Ben, the other men had already begun firing before he even decided on a target. Ben picked a fat dead creature running near the head of the second wave and took aim. His rifle jumped as he put a round through the thing's skull and watched its body hit the pavement, rolling from its momentum.

One of the men beside Ben was armed with an as-sault rifle and it chattered continuously as he leaned over the edge and emptied its clip into the crowd already at-tacking the door below. The dead turned their faces up-wards howling at the men on the roof as death rained down on them.

Ben fired off two more shots before he got to his feet. "There's too many!" he yelled. "The door will never hold."

As Ben turned to head back inside, the sound of squealing tires tore his attention back out towards the streets. He watched in disbelief as Terry's patrol car came streaking out of the night. It looked as if the car was doing close to a hundred miles per hour as struck the ranks of the dead. Then the night was lit up as the car exploded in the center of the street sending flames and shrapnel fly-ing. Ben jerked his arm over his face on reflex.

A truck plowed through the street in the wake of the patrol car ramming its blazing, wreckage aside. The truck bounced over the corpses of the creatures below and shook as the dead left still moving in the main street in front of the hall leapt onto its sides and threw themselves in front of it trying to bring the vehicle to a halt. The truck man-aged to make it all the way to the hall's door and the driver arced it sideways skidding to a stop which put the truck's mass directly against that of the doorway into the hall. The driver kicked open his door and knocked a dead thing from its feet in the process. When Ben saw who the driver was, as the man below hopped onto the top of the truck's cab, his face broke into a smile.

"Terry!" Ben yelled. He dropped back into a firing po-sition and motioned to the other men on the roof. "Give him some cover!" Ben ordered. "Robert, get down there and get the door open for him now!" Robert raced down the stairs.

The hall's doors opened inward and Robert tugged them open after tearing off the small amount of boarding that had been nailed into place before the dead had made their attack. Terry jumped down from the top of the truck into the hall as Robert and several men shoved the doors closed in front of the dead who followed Terry. Terry threw his weight against the door helping Robert and the men to hold the doorway closed. The truck prevented too many of the dead from attacking the doorway at once and luck was with them. Others from the crowd of the living gathered within the hall came forward and started hammering the door's fortifications back into place. The pounding on the door did not stop but things had grown quieter outside the building. Ben came down the stairs from the roof and headed straight for Terry. He threw his arms about him and squeezed him like a mad man. "How in the hell did you pull off that stunt with the car?"

"The old stick on the gas, grenade in the front seat routine," Terry laughed.

"You really shook things up out there. The dead have pulled back for the moment, at least most of them. You took a lot of them out."

"That was the plan," Terry grinned.

"Uh, guys," Robert ventured.

Terry and Ben turned their attention to him.

"I hate to break up your reunion but Gordon's back."

❧❧

As Ben told Terry what little he knew of what had happened to Terry's former deputy, Terry stood peeking through the cracks of the hall's board up front window. Ben could see that Terry was hurt at the loss of his friend.

"What the hell is he doing?" Terry asked as Gordon took a few steps closer to the town hall and he lost sight of Gordon's decaying form as it passed behind the truck Terry had parked in front of the entrance way.

"He's not like the others Terry," Ben warned, "Gordon may be dead but somehow he can still think."

Terry heard the truck outside crank up. "Can he drive too?" Terry asked.

"Oh, shit," Ben muttered as the men inside the hall saw the truck back up and pull away from the main door. Its tires squealed as the thing that had been Gordon whirled it around to face the doorway.

Someone near Terry broke out a window and started

shooting. It was too late though. The truck roared and
lunged forward. Terry and Ben leapt from its path as the
truck tore through the hall's door, ripping open the wall.
Splinters and pieces of wood exploded inward as the truck
crashed into the hall.

The interior of the hall was chaos. Men moved to take
positions to try to hold out the dead outside as the creatures realized what Gordon had done and rushed into the
hall after the truck. Other men fought desperately to try
to move the women and the few children still in Cobble
into the hall's basement.

The dead came flowing into the building like a flood.
Gunshots thundered all around Terry and people were
screaming everywhere. Terry looked around for Ben. They
had been separated as they dodged the incoming truck.
He spotted Ben lying near the opposite wall. Ben wasn't
moving. A long shard of timber pinned Ben's mangled form
to the floor. Terry cursed and threw his rifle aside. He
jerked his sidearm from its holster and turned to face
where the truck had came to a stop in a pile of rubble. A
dead creature jumped at him from his left. He spun around
smashing the butt of his .38 into its face. Its nose was
knocked up and into the thing's brain from the blow and
the thing toppled out of his way.

Terry saw Gordon climb out of the truck. The deputy's
eyes met his own. Gordon's blood smeared lips parted in
the semblance of a smile. "T-err-y," the thing wailed.

Terry didn't bother to aim as Gordon charged him.
He fired four times before Gordon reached him. The first
round shattered Gordon's left shoulder. Two struck the
deputy in the chest but without enough force to knock
him back. Terry's last round fired at almost point blank
impaled the creature's left eye and sent chunks of tissue
and tiny pieces of bone flying out of the back of the thing's
head. Terry caught Gordon's corpse in his arms as the
once again lifeless body careened into him and Gordon's
momentum knocked Terry from his feet. Terry kicked
Gordon's remains off of him and got back to his feet. The
dead outnumbered the living inside the hall now. Very few
of the hall's defenders were left alive. The door to the hall's

basement stood ajar and he saw Tim trying to force it closed against the two howling creatures who fought to get inside.

Terry made for the doorway. As he ran he emptied his handgun into the two creatures Tim struggled against. They dropped out of his way and he reached the door himself and knocked it open. As he rolled inside, Tim tried to slam it shut once more but a gray, maggot infested hand managed to slide inside keeping the door cracked open.

There were still two other men left alive in the basement. Both were armed with assault rifles from the hall's supplies. They stood ready, waiting on Tim to fail.

"Tim, let them in," Terry ordered, motioning for the two men to open up with their weapons as the door was pushed inward and Tim dove out of the way. For a few seconds, just as Terry had hoped the entrance way became a meat grinder. The two men held their fingers on the triggers of their weapons until the chattering turned to a series of clicks. As soon as the bullets stopped, Terry hopped up grabbing the door. He shoved it back against the ranks of the dead. But his plan had backfired.

The dead were now piled too high in the entrance way for him to even hope that he could get the door shut and more of the dead still fought to press through over the bodies of their fellows.

Terry heard someone screaming from the depths of the basement below. "Oh lord, Terry! They're down here too!" he heard Tim screaming. From the corner of his eye, Terry saw a man in military uniform with red foam bubbling from his mouth come racing up the basement steps at the two men hurrying to reload their rifles. The military dressed creature grabbed the closer of the two men and sunk its teeth into the flesh of his neck. Blood spurted over the thing's hungry lips.

Terry turned, forgetting about defending the hopeless doorway, and rushed the creature. He tackled it and pulled it to the ground. His fist rose and fell in an unrelenting rhythm pounding into the thing's blood smeared face. He heard the door above him make a "thunk" sound as the mass of the dead finally managed to force it open and come through. Terry looked down the steps into the mass of women and the few scattered younger children gathered in the shelter of the basement below, and he knew it was over. Their eyes had no fight or hope left within them and there were hundreds of the dead above waiting to rend and tear their flesh. Terry felt hands clawing at him from behind. He heard himself screaming then as he lifted from his feet and dragged up the steps out the basement by his hair. The last thing Terry saw were dirt-covered fingers as they reached over the top of his head and dug into his eyes. His only thought was of Amy. He mentally pleaded for her safety. His last thought was a simple *I love you* that he tried to will her to hear.

Minutes later, the only sound that could be heard inside Cobble's massive town hall was the gnawing of teeth on flesh and bones as at last the dead had their feast.

⌘

Drake and his company of Christina, Amy, and the children had emerged from the cave. They headed out to the East in search of a saver place. Christina's face was a mask of pain but she held the pistol Drake had given her in hands, fully loaded and ready. According to Drake, it wouldn't be of any use against the thing that was coming for them but it certainly would work against the dead. Drake walked away from them, his face stone.

Christina kept the children huddled together as they marched but they didn't make it far. From the edges of the clearing they stood in the dead came out of the trees surrounding them. She had no idea where they had come from but there were over a dozen of them. Christina threw herself between them and the children. "Drake!," she yelled, taking aim at the closest creature as they rushed her but he didn't seem to be able to hear her. His thoughts were focused on the dead things' master. They were too fast for her in her weakened condition. They poured over her washing her to the ground under their snapping teeth as more stepped out the woods surrounding the children. Christina screamed for Drake, for God, and fell silent as her blood spilt onto the grass as gnashing teeth and grimy fingers tore her apart and opened her insides to the night air.

The children and Amy shrieked and howled as the dead grabbed them up one by one and carried them back the way they had come to the clearing and their approaching master.

～∾

Drake had realized that this showdown was inevitable. He'd known on some deeper level for years. Even as a child, he'd felt the call of a higher purpose, something luring him to the path he was on. It was something he knew, instinctively, and could not be shirked from—too much was at stake and hanging in the balance.

In the small clearing east of the caves where Amy and the children were waiting behind him, he gazed up to the sky. The lightning was vivid and stretched across the sky like silver veins; it formed a strange luminous web, one he felt he could not escape or hide from. His legs were braced, fists clenched, and his skin tingled from the electrical charge in the air and this final moment of truth; here in the moments, the limbo, between dark and dawn when all critical battles were lost and won.

And now, He was coming. The wind picked up outside the perimeter of the clearing but did not bluster inside. And then the demon was there at the opposite side of the clearing, darkly shrouded, and filled with silent hatred.

But suddenly he heard sounds from behind him. Crouched and bowed the undead were dragging something into the clearing: Amy, Caleb, the little ones: Ingrid and Isaac, and the others, unconscious, into the center of the clearing to be laid on the ground as the spoils of their war. Drake heard their frail heartbeats struggling, straining to hold on to the life that was being drained by the dark figure. Drake waited. He expected to intuit what to do, how to counter his enemy... Nothing surfaced, but he could feel its push within him, searching for a way out. It grew and boiled, but could find no release as the cloaked man glided forward and bent to take Amy's hair in his hand and pull her head back exposing her pale throat. He stared at Drake, challenging him to make a move.

Drake's teeth ground together. Inside him, pressure was building to an intolerable pitch as if the storm was inside him; if only he knew what to do...he concentrated but could not leash the wildness. He felt as if it would tear him apart.

The demon raised his hand and the lightning bolts flew to him from the overhead sky, strange blue and green matrix that swirled in the air, surrounding them in the circle. He seemed to be savoring the moment, taking his time.

In the east, the sky was loosing its darkness. The demon grinned; then with a wave of his shadowy arm, the night sky drifted to the east and covered the yellow-orange tinge of birth, stifling the light, suffocating it. The circle of lightning stopped its rotating and with a crackling strike raced out from the circle into the forest and beyond, engulfing the trees and ground in a fire as rapid as wind. And still Drake could not control the forces within him. His eyes closed with the strain; his hands shook. And when he opened them again, Amy knelt before him, clutching her throat with both hands as if trying to pry invisible hands from it. Gasping she reached and pulled at Drake's legs with her rigid desperate fingers. She pulled at his legs until he knelt before her, the inferno raging around them. "I'm sorry. I'm so sorry," he choked. He had failed her. Failed everyone. She clutched at him, tried to speak, but couldn't. And Drake hugged her to him, the tempest inside him swallowing up the both of them until they rocked together on the ground from the force of it and finally he felt the ease of her arms, felt the slump of her body against his, and knew she was gone. No longer did he feel the life-thread of the children. They too had been overcome. His path had abandoned him. The pressure inside him began to ebb away, to be replaced with remorse that was ten times more crippling. Oh, for the chance to do it again—was there a sign he didn't heed? A whisper he didn't hear? Still holding Amy's body against him, he looked up into the black skies and released his anger the only way he could: with silent open-mouthed screams.

The demon strode forward. Such sweet pain washed from his timeless enemy, this half-breed of flesh and divine being, this archangel of humanity; how would he taste when enclosed into his own darkness? Sucked in, corroded with evil, forever joined as puppet to its master...

The pain was splitting him into shreds. *Desolation is my name. I am nothing...All I'll ever be...is nothing.* And finally he bent, laid Amy on the ground; he wasn't fit to touch her, never had been. His hand hovered over her face, the pale green eyes open and staring to the sky, once more he wanted to touch her. He ached to close her eyes to all this misery that had been her life, and close her eyes to his face...his failure...he couldn't bear it... But instead he raised his hand to his own cheek, where something warm trickled and slid to the corner of his mouth—it tasted salty. And he gathered the wetness onto his fingers and gasped with awe. It glimmered as it streaked across his palm and onto Amy's face.

The demon gasped. We don't shed tears...

And the teardrop slipped from Amy's face to the ground...

"It's impossible! We don't shed—"

The lightning stopped. The demon whirled around to face the east where the darkness was rolling back upon itself as if reversing time. "It's impossible I tell you!" he roared to the sky.

The ground trembled, faintly at first, then forcibly it quaked. Rain began to fall in great torrents and when they touched the demon he began to moan and shriek, trying to wipe them from his face, his hands, his black cloak. His eyes sizzled in their sockets as smoke billowed from his sleeves, his feet, and finally every part of him. Until finally all that was left where he stood was mud and ash.

Drake felt a tug on his knee. Amy's rain-glistening face was looking up at him. For a moment neither was capable of words. But then her lips parted and slowly she said, "Not nothing, *Everything.*"

Ingrid and Isaac stirred first, then Marcus and the others, rubbing their eyes as if asleep for a hundred years. Drake motioned them into his arms. Isaac, wide-eyed, climbed onto Drake's lap, looked up and plucked his thumb from his mouth, "bad man gone." Ingrid, who had leaned her head against Drake's shoulder, now leaned forward and kissed her younger brother's cheek. "Yes, he's gone," she said, and then she pointed behind Isaac, "Look! The sun's coming up!"

The sun radiated through the evaporating clouds, casting a honey-warm glow. The fires had ceased abruptly with Cryten's eradication; the burnt stalks of great oaks and giant elms stood smoldering in the prismic rays.

"Christina didn't make it. She died trying to save me and the children from—from those monsters"

"Shh-shh," Drake's fingertip lightly pressed against her lips. "She'll always be remembered, but we have to move forward. We have to let the past go in order to rebuild the future, for the children. Especially for the children."

Epilogue

Many years had passed since the night Michael Drake had stood against the demonic thing known as Cryten and the dead walked on Cobble Island, but Amy would never forget those times. She remembered all of it as if it were yesterday. Her nightmares were still haunted by images of her father's corpse, eyeless and sprawled out on the floor of the town hall, lying in a sea of bodies of people she had known and loved. Everyone on Cobble who hadn't been with Michael and under his protection that night had been killed by the dead-things the demon had conjured up to do its will. The loss of her father nearly tore her apart but Drake somehow kept her from falling apart. He kept them all together that day as the dead were buried for a final time.

The dead-things themselves had vanished when Drake had taken Cryten's life but even so, life hadn't been easy on Cobble during the first years after the battle. Everyday had been a struggle to move on and rebuild. So many things had been lost to them. All of the survivors except she, herself, and Michael had been children and as a group they lacked a good many skills. It was like learning how to live all over again. Gone were the "golden" days of the human race with technology and all its comforts. But they had survived. They learned how to plant and grow crops on the island like their parents before them and they learned how to fish. They learned how to do things they never imagined they could with Michael's help and from the books he gathered from the homes across the island.

The children grew older and married and soon there was new life on Cobble once more.

Amy pulled herself out of her memories and looked down at the dirt. She was old now and her auburn hair long since turned gray but she still managed to help in growing the crops for the winter season. She picked up some dirt from the garden bed she sat in and let it run through her hands before she planted the last seed at the end of the row she was working on. She could hear the distant yells of Caleb's children at play in the fields while they worked. She watched over them during the days when Caleb took out his boat off the coast of Cobble to fish since his wife Ingrid had grown up to be the island's sole person with any kind of skill at engineering other than Drake and was often away on trips to the mainland to gather supplies for the continued expansion of the community the last survivors of the "dark days" had become.

There still had been no word at all from the outside world and Ingrid and her group of scavengers who did visit the mainland had never seen any trace of evidence that the people of Cobble weren't alone in the world. Drake had told them all they were alone time and time again but no one ever gave up hope.

A shadow fell over her, blocking the harsh rays of the mid-day sun from the bare, wrinkled skin of her back left uncovered by the tank top she wore. She looked up to see Drake standing behind her. He barely looked older than he did on the day she had met him. Somehow the years had passed him by without leaving a trace of their passage. He claimed it was heritage that kept him from aging though he refused to say any more about it. During his battle with Cryten, he had at last discovered beyond any shadow of doubt, that he too, was not human, at least not fully. He held out a glass of cool water to her and she could see the love for her burning brightly in his eyes. If her growing older and withered on the outside had ever bothered Drake, he'd never shown it. The love they shared seemed eternal and immune to such petty things.

She took the glass and sipped at it. "Looks like things are getting better," she laughed.

Drake grinned, squatting beside her to place an arm on her shoulders. He leaned over to her and gave her a quick kiss. "Better all the time," he agreed.

After Words

By Eric S. Brown

In the words of my friend Scott Nicholson, "This is the fun part of the book for the writer, but (a part) that can be dreadfully tedious for some readers". This is the part where the author shares a bit of the "whys" and "hows" of the book.

Writing Cobble was a long, hard journey for me. I consider myself to be a short story author *not* a novelist but since I first began to sale my stories on a regular basis there have been people in my life, my wife loudest among them, who have told me that I need to write a "book". With three paperback collection deals, four chapbooks, two e-books already behind me and two more chapbooks in the works, I honestly felt I *had* written books already. I just didn't get what they were saying. It took a long to sink in.

In some ways, I had proven myself worthy of the term writer but was I really an "author" without a novel to my credit? The voices of those people told me I wasn't and when I re-examined myself and my career, taking a look at writers I admire like H.P. Lovecraft and David Drake, I decided to give it a shot. I have never been a writer who handles working in the long form well. More to the point, outside a few novellas I had never even tried it. I knew if I was going to do this and create a novel I was going to need a really good story idea and help from another writer who was better at some of the things I am not so wonderful at.

The idea was the hard part. I knew the book simply had to be a zombie novel because, God bless them, those flesh eating undead monsters were the things that inspired me and gave me the passion to write in the first place. At the same time, I knew I wanted and needed the book to have at least a loose military feel to it because that's the other thing I enjoy writing almost as much. Mixing the two without falling into cliché these days is not an easy task. The idea for Cobble came from the fact that I had already written it to a degree. During my first year as a writer, I wrote a screenplay with the same title and very similar plot which I had never even thought about trying to market. It was an idea I loved and something deeper too on a personal level. It was kind an homage to all those films sitting in my study that my wife won't let me display in the living room, a good, fun, "end of the world" tale of death and hope intermingled.

So with the idea in my head, I went out searching for a co-author. I knew it had to be someone with talent and someone that I had never worked with before so it would all be fresh and different. In August, 2003, I met Susanne Brydenbaugh in person at the Horrorfind convention in Baltimore. I had read her work and knew her to be a rising star of dark fiction and I knew her work was somewhat deeper than my own. She really added an element of feeling to her characters that was beyond me. After returning from the con, I wrote her up via e-mail and pitched my idea to her. She thought it was worthy of investing her time in and so we started.

The process of writing Cobble took eight painful months of bouncing chapters back and forth through e-mail. Somehow we survived it though and things really appeared to work out well. She added things to the storyline that I had never considered and took my ideas and helped me develop them far beyond anything I ever expected. Don't get me wrong, we had a great time writing this novel but if anyone ever tells you writing isn't work, look them dead in the eyes and laugh in their face.

Cobble is the best thing I have ever produced in all three years I have been plugging away with the pen and I owe a good deal of that to Susanne. There is something more meaningful about Cobble too, to me, that no critic, reviewer, or sales statement can ever take from me. Cobble is my first novel. If I keep waking up tomorrow and tomorrow and tomorrow and write four more "books", it doesn't change the fact that this book represents a turning point in both my life and career. It is something I never thought I could do or even dreamed of doing (honestly) if my wife, friends, and some editors hadn't kept hounding me about it.

So to you readers, I hope you enjoyed the book and to you, Mr. Romero, my inspiration still, thank you for the nightmares.

And The Dead Shall Rise

By Eric S. Brown

Chris ducked further into the brush surrounding the road as the police cruiser slowed. An officer leaned out of the passenger side window, shining a hand lamp across the tree line. Maggots slithered in and out of his pale, rotting cheeks..

Chris held his breath and prayed that his luck would hold. The light moved over his face, burning his eyes, and moved on past him into the trees.

"Nothing here." The officer said in the hollow, cold voice of the dead. The cruiser picked up speed and disappeared over the nearby hill.

Chris started to breathe again, mopping at the sweat on his brow with the sleeve of his filthy and tattered flannel shirt. It had been close, too close. Only God knew what would've happened had the officers discovered him. Chris had heard stories that the last "Breathers" were being herded up, gathered into breeding centers so that they weren't forced completely into extinction as the society of the dead took their place as the rulers of the Earth.

Everything had changed so much over the past year; Chris still sometimes wondered if he was stuck inside one of his own nightmares. In the before times, he had been a powerful man, the owner of a chain of grocery stores which stretched from one coast of America to the other. He'd had money, women, respect, but none of that mattered now. Like anyone else left alive, he was merely food—an animal to be hunted and killed.

Chris jumped out of the brush onto the road and took off at a run in the opposite direction the cruiser had gone. His breath came in ragged gasps as he pushed his body beyond its limits. He remembered the days when the dead were slow pitiful things, lumbering around like mindless automatons. If only the world had awoken sooner to the danger they posed, they'd never have been allowed to evolve into what they were. Now, they spoke, drove cars, used weapons and did all the things "Breathers" used to.

Chris had not seen another living soul in weeks and he didn't know how much longer he could go on. He felt so very tired. The past few months, he'd managed to survive more through luck than skill.

Chris came to a jarring halt in the middle of the road as he saw a house up ahead. There were lights on inside it and smoke rolled out of its rock chimney towards the stars. Chris was not naive enough to believe that there could be real people inside in its walls, but a gnawing curiosity made him approach it.

He ducked off the side of the road into the trees and crept towards the house's lawn. He could see someone or something moving above the sink through its kitchen window. Chris sank to his belly and crawled across the dark yard. He dug his .38 revolver from his jacket pocket, carrying it openly as he crawled.

He reached the side of the house and got to his feet leaning against the wall, careful to stay out view of the window. He could hear the sounds of leftovers being scraped off a plate into the sink. Chris snuck around the side of the house searching for another window, wanting desperately to get a look inside.

The lights were off in the living room as he peeked through its window, only the dim glow of a TV screen lit the room. A man sat in a recliner watching the screen intently. The man's flesh was gray and decayed. At his feet sat a young boy. The child paid no attention to the TV, staring directly out the window at Chris.

Chris jumped back as if he'd been physically struck but when no alarm sounded from within the house; he found the nerve to peer inside once more. Then he noticed the boy's eyes. He looked into the child's empty sockets and watched as a worm worked it way free and fell to the wooden floor.

The tiny thing began to cry. The man yelled something Chris couldn't quite make out and got to his feet. He scooped the child up in his arms and yelled again. A woman entered the room from the kitchen, her long blonde hair matted to her scalp with blood and pus from an ancient wound on her forehead. She rested her hands on her hips and scowled at the man. Chris thought he heard her say something about bedtime.

Chris ducked below the window. The woman despite being dead had eyes that still saw. He remained motionless until the voices disappeared deeper into the house.

Chris felt sick, leaning over as he nearly vomited onto the grass. He'd never imagined the dead could really live like this. They were supposed to be monsters-hungry, evil things waiting to tear the flesh off your bones. Not a family tucking their child in for the night.

The bright lights of the cruiser topped the hill heading back toward Chris and the house. He stood in plain view of the road and there was no way he could cross the distance to the trees before the cruiser reached the house.

Inside his mind whatever remnants of sanity survived gave way. He charged out onto the road in front of the cruiser shouting at the top of his lungs.

"Jesus!" The officer at the wheel screamed as he swerved the vehicle to the left narrowly avoiding Chris. His partner snatched up the car radio. "This is car 71. We have a "breather" down by the Peterson farm on route 106. Requesting back-up!"

Chris aimed and fired several times at the thing behind the wheel. The windshield shattered spraying shards of glass into the car as the bullets tore into the officer's chest. The thing leapt out of the car as blackish goo leaked from the wounds staining the front of its uniform. "Drop your weapon!" It shouted pointing its own handgun at

Chris.

Chris turned to flee back towards the house as the front door swung open. The father-creature stood there with a 12 gauge leveled at Chris's stomach. He saw his own fear and hatred reflected in the thing's dull, glazed over eyes. The night shook as the 12 gauge thundered. The blast knocked Chris off his feet, his intestines spilling onto the dirt as he fell.

The officer ran over to stand above him pointing his pistol into Chris's face. Chris smelt the officer's ripe state of decay as drops of black pus dripped from its wounds onto the bare skin of his face. The last thing Chris saw was the barrel explode with light before the bullet ripped through his brain.

The mother-thing ran out of the house, shoving her husband aside as she made her way onto the lawn. "Oh God!" She wailed seeing Chris's corpse sprawled before her. Blood dripped from Chris's forehead onto the asphalt as his body twitched, growing cold. The officer turned to her, a smile on his withered lips, saying, "It's all right ma'am. Everything's okay. The monster is dead now."

About the Authors

Eric S. Brown is a 30-year-old writer living in Western, North Carolina. His works include the paperback collections: *Walking Nightmares, Space Stations and Graveyards, Dying Days,* and *Portals of Terror,* the chapbooks: *As We All Break Down, Viruses & Vamps, Dark Karma, Bad Mojo, Flashes of Death, Zombies: The War Stories, Still Dead* and *Blood Rain,* as well as the e-books *Poisoned Graves* and *Quantum Nightmares.*

His short fiction has been published over two hundred times in a wide array of both print and on-line markets like *The Book of Dark Wisdom, The Eternal Night, Alien Skin, Story House, The Edge, Jupiter SF, Black Petals, Post Mortem, Blood Lust, Cyberpulp Magazine,* and many, many more.

Eric's work has also appeared in anthologies like *The Blackest Death* Volumes I and II, *The Undead, Fantasies, Of Flesh and Hunger,* and *Monsters Ink* among others.

When not writing himself, he can often be found spending time with his lovely and supportive wife (Shanna), reading authors like David Drake and John Ringo, or watching horror films like *Dawn of the Dead.*

Susanne Brydenbaugh is the author of over 80 short stories and poems published in the small press.
Her most current work can be found in *Gothic Net, Aoife's Kiss, Black Petals, Would That It Were, Permutations: The Journal of Unsettling Fiction, The City Morgue* magazine, and following anthologies: *Cemetary Poets: Grave Offerings, Atrocitas Aqua, Femmes De La Brume: Women of Speculative Fiction.*

The Italian Publisher, Ghost Edizioni and German publisher, UBooks, will translate (in both Italian and German) two of her short stories in the anthology: *Amazzoni,* and in the Young Adult anthology: *Toys in the Attic,* scheduled for October/November 2004.

She is completing her novel, *Midnight Cry,* a dark, gothic fantasy of a real ghost town that refuses to be inhabited.

Other than writing and reading voraciously, she enjoys the outdoors, craves music, and is a classic car enthusiast.

She shares her home with two German Shepherds and a weird-ass breed of a cat in the southern U.S.

Her website can be found at: www.mywriterstooth.com

The ChroMagic Series
by Piers Anthony

1,000 years ago Earth colonized the planet Charm. But the population of Charm is now far removed from their ancient ancestors. Technology has been lost over the years but the people have something better--Magic!

Key to Havoc
ChroMagic Series, Book One

Once again, Mr Anthony creates a complex world unlike anything we might imagine.
—Amanda Killgore, Scribes World

Oh my lord, this was a fantastic book!!
—Chris Roeszler, Amazon Reviewer

Trade Paperback • ISBN 0-9723670-6-3
Hardcover • ISBN 0-9723670-7-1
eBook • ISBN 1-59426-000-1

Key To Chroma
ChroMagic Series, Book Two

Chroma continues to fascinate, making readers anxious for the final book in the trilogy.
—Amanda Killgore, Scribes World

Trade Paperback • ISBN 1-59426-018-4
Hardcover • ISBN 1-59426-017-6
eBook • ISBN 1-59426-019-2

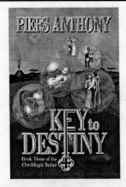

Key to Destiny
ChroMagic Series, Book Three

Piers Anthony is one of those authors who can perform magic with the ordinary.
—A Reader's Guide to Science Fiction

Trade Paperback • ISBN 1-59426-044-3
Hardcover • ISBN 1-59426-043-5
eBook • ISBN 1-59426-045-1

Books by Elaine Corvidae

Wolfkin
Lord of Wind and Fire, Book One
A kingdom on the eve of war. A queen held captive. A land in turmoil. A shape-changer's heart.

Wolfkin is a superb fantasy shapeshifter romance that will keep you turning the pages.
—Debora Hosey, Romance Readers Connection

Trade Paperback • ISBN 1-59426-055-9
Hardcover • ISBN 1-59426-054-0
eBook • ISBN 1-59426-053-2

The Crow Queen
Lord of Wind and Fire, Book Two
Vengeance. Passion. Magic. Power.

Ms. Corvidae shows yet again her penchant for weaving engrossing fantasy tales.
—Kelley A. Hartsell, July 2004

Trade Paperback • ISBN 1-59426-058-3
Hardcover • ISBN 1-59426-057-5
eBook • ISBN 1-59426-056-7

Dragon's Son
Lord of Wind and Fire, Book Three
Lost to his friends, Yozerf must also make his way back to Kellsjard.

For the lover of fantasy and fantasy romance, this book is definitely for you!
—Amy L. Turpin, Timeless Tales

Trade Paperback • ISBN 1-59426-061-3
Hardcover • ISBN 1-59426-060-5
eBook • ISBN 1-59426-059-1

LaVergne, TN USA
25 January 2010
171069LV00001B/19/A